A hotel is defined by its inhabitants

CALLAS: WHO NEEDS THE MET?

The Hare

Glykeria Patramani

Once, a father hunted all morning long down by the creek. When the sun came up, he hit a hare, brought it home, and left it in the sink. The mother flayed the hare, cooked a stew with shallots and sewed the tail on a string so as for the cats to play. The child ate some of the stew and bit the pellet accidentally left inside. His tooth cracked and his mouth, like the sink, filled with blood. Now, every time he eats hare, a man strokes his chin and remembers his parents.

Four Poems

Felicity & **Two types of the same return** & **Moss** & **Sketch for a**

Imogen Cassels

Felicity

Morning irising; some things are no good, where
you forgot she wore her legs like that, a symmetry
I never heard of. Best in paradise at night alone
or fen coe (this tristesse); a *bleu néant* that's inbuilt,
slipping into difficulty or easy-access grace like
salt in a wound. Spirit is a bone; hail is cashmere;
this feels chic and not nervous, now and very typically
cyanotype. Whenever I'll be afraid / of the obscurity
of water *this moment is apocalyptic and a type of heaven*,
with marmalade. Or blood honey. Seasons new wear
lightly throw off your clothes spread wide awhile—Oh,
where? Like Ink or Charcoal, that's a readymade or just
citational beatitude. And like spring for furs reasonable,
you could do that with anything, couldn't you?

/

another en train de Harlow which resembles
   fashion landscape almost—anyway it's minimal
with decent light. a heroin named Rosalind,
   Ophelia a cut of dress (the corset's see-through
you luminous). like virginity or any threshold strung
   to tenderness or somehow held: once you
have worn these things you can't return; it feels like
   nothing, or heaven, silk-lined. I find it's true.
I want to marry you but I'd rather have a pair
   of Miu Miu cat eyes or more black fox. blessure,
a sacrifice you signed for prior to waking. I haven't
   stitches yet, which retains inevitability, sexy,
without coy traces. *live free die strong* should make us lithe
   and various, advancing ahead while fumbling
around in the dark, a motto for bad reading made
   reparative. and when I arrive, then, honey-like-heather:
your eyes are nothing like the sun in Hackney

Two types of the same return

but in a beetle by mining exos and drops
of rain and bush dust
                                        it's beautiful to be
trim or take lines up to the loaded moon /
in a naïve swoop tanglier. "these are
the glass minutes of my eyes, or like
I could eat twice as many flowers as you
I'm trailing off, crush-crush.

                                        it's
January it's almost spring every starlit fence
is tiny. the primroses saying know know know
or hello!,
     opened vein or
                         do you even have roses?
                         the size of a continent.
my mother is a rowan tree I'm so conspicuous without.
artifice enough for any hope lopsided,
your means of *soutiens*,
to Paris in our times.

                                        comprehending.
and the magpies—five—skirmishing
won't console hurt. motherofpearl inlay me
all across my back.   stained glass
whatever.   thousands of bats fly out of a cave //
I love art.   with all the accidental *tendresse* of holding out
a mobile calling "it's for you—
                                                  forwent something
almost being said:
                                        my breastbone is a bat
put out of temper; I am become a shrine;
sad flush of every demi-form;
it catches like a sycamore

Moss

dizzy weepies with repeat oh morning hazel
she's so suspended third so autopilot harmony
wish if grief would label itself to imagine
repeating a summer again like circle at least
six or whatever unknowing what a window
means there is a hot line of fabric on my back
and the centre of my lips is a heart I've such
an amount of nothing in my pocket you'd
never listen without is hell oh hiya ilya ilya ilya
there's no fix for never having your siskin
daughter furling out of place well uplight
blossom this the sun damage blissing kate's
narrow chest blueshirt new in for may
the luminous possibility of a child

Sketch for a

I can't believe you expect me to be beautiful
through all of this. I mean, I expect myself.
It's difficult: blazer April pink gelée champagne
liner yacht foreclosed a blue prow. Google maps
at night. Do with frosting disparage for a thicket
brackish throw oystering. Accidental happiness
the slight the company she kept: it's a small form
to gather; you could fold or pleat me. There are
so joys still: a pigeon breast's diagonal of bright
searedness; cherry wood; chips a gin and tonic, sinew.
Well that summer it was hot—it glowed—and I
had started bleeding—like when you cornered
the avant-garde, after the symposium, and asked him
what would come next and he just shrugged
and said "love

Seven Pages

Will Oldham

When I was a dreamer

when I wasn't dreaming
thi ng s were fine
smoke a cigarette on
my own time
able-body baby
was with me
gotta love your baby
completely

everybody 's failing
their own test
always redefining
what they do best
n o one is the same
from start to last
and the ~~friends~~ of the ~~future~~ are coming
a~~in't th e friends of the past~~
will go by fast

and I think it's funny
to talk with one
who's failed me whollyly
so undon e
sits ~~with~~ here with me
~~with an idiot's grin~~ where I have seen
and tries to while I try to figure
what ~~did him in~~
ruined him

was a man that loved me
and I liked him
but I couldn't take him
as more than a friend
now I never see him
just as well
jammin on the fact that
one man fell

but events are leading
to a class

G# B6m

I think I had a dog
the things we true were taught
loyal torn from our heart

bridge needed

Its now so soft under foot

we sleep more than we sleep

if god could make me cry
Id run along the water

~~wouldn't do anything well~~

play with it while you have hands
a desperate lack of demands
I cant offer a thing
better than ~~death~~, so take it!
dying

one feels strange first

(C) (D) (G)

This is better, that one does
Her own mask as she may, though in the night he calls/falls
I am sorry to bury you

(G) (D) (G)

Oh! token travails, in other worlds
the clouds puzzle the eyes on them
But who shall seek another world wanders — (G) (D) (C)
among the mighty devils of mal → G
There is no home that's not for you → C

This is better, that one does
Her Own mask as she may though in the night he calls/falls
I am sorry to bury you
(I am sorry to sully you)

There is no love for this shovel
which returns more than it turns
Thus peforming is of no ill -
that shameful eye, syrum infused
motions you, you lowering us all
to the Will.

C D G × 2

Gone like the last one, there is enough for this
Gone like the last one, there is enough for this.

D G D G
D G Em C

scrap the outfit
hand me the keys to your car
if I leave before it is light
I'll be around when you are

CAL'S SONG

~~I~~ don't want ~~any~~one to call my own I would have to push away
No sweetheart to ~~lie and be~~tray push away
one To not be there when I get home
~~And make~~ another evening gray ~~and awful~~
making just emptying

O lord I will be good in heaven
Call me to sit at your right side
I ~~It~~'s only earthly sin
Because it's earth I'm in I do not
And I stand in my doing and ~~don't~~ hide

feeling
What has made this in my mind
What came to bring me here? what even allowed my body to be here?
Well I believe in justice kind , right punishment is what I fear
And that's just what ~~I fear~~ bonny old me does fear

with, that I've come to
For everything ~~I~~ fear and loathe many times
I've done to one already
And quake at night to telltale noise
Of justice creeping stealthyly
what I know must be

O lord I will be good in heaven
Call me to sit at your right side
It's only earthly sin
Because it's earth I'm in
And I stand in my doing and don't hide

Lord your your
~~God will~~ take ~~his~~ stranglehold
And squeeze the living out of breath
Beat the smiles from my mouth
+ break The spring from my ~~stepping~~ free step
The very tone my own name rings
Inside my head
Will be ~~dulled~~ when ~~he~~ silenced you
Kill~~s~~ ~~the good in~~ me dead
put the life in me to bed

~~Because I have asked for it~~

O lord I will be good in heaven
Call me to sit at your right side
It's only earthly sin
Because it's earth I'm in
And I stand in my doing and don't hide

G

ROYALTY

ere's what I found ~~hidden~~ that gone in the glass
worm, an ice cube, permission to pass
bitter taste with a sweet finish
help me up and to replenish

ere's what I heard just outside
e motor start for an engine ride
d the call t~~o come~~ from my lady's ~~voice~~ tongue
~~hich when sounded depletes all choice~~ reaches my ears, revs me up and I commence to come

+C, G

yalty the royal we
ve struck it off again
cing through the country lane
e ~~thing~~ we've fallen in
yally she next to we
all the crown I own
til we crown ourselves again when we come rolling home

god's my witness there she goes
contained by heavy clothes
e keep ~~our~~ my voice~~s~~ to a murmer
sperate not to do harm to her

w would that reflect upon us?
our friends are sure to leave us
t for now we are contented
walk togetherly resplendent

horus — A

not. verse — A

chorus

friends)

gypsy limeric / flood

E♭ E x3

banana blood

well I came upon a spider
who gruffly said to me
if I could handle happiness
he'd show me how to be
he said you've got inside of you
a dew that's holy-fine
a liquid form so sweet and warm
I shouldnt harbor Mine A → E
walk over to that woman
with the big black hi-heeled shoe
and hold her very closely
and hold her fast and true
I know it sounds far fetched but dear
a spider told me how
to make the love you're drinking here
the joy that we know now
I promise you our life forever
the world well-off can screw
and I will share my banan blood with you F#m E

share my banana blood
share my banana blood
share my banana blood with you.
the world thinks it's well-off without us
the world well-off can screw
because I'll share my banana blood with you

x3, stop, 1 more ...

you know what
world
can
because I'm
sharing
bana
b
with
yo
y

she leaned back on the wood
and she closed her
eyes

saying quietly
as she went
to sleep

GRADGUD

sb WGdD

we are two children
we have ~~behaved~~ acted foolishly
when could we possibly
o when could we possibly

only every summer
then only if you know
o I know I know I only know you
and always this will be true
living on the memory of this love
memory is knowledge dove
~~and with that, ... tried~~
~~she read me ... I had ...~~ ~~as her gingerfoot tugged~~
~~her off shore - ta!~~
don't let anyone see us
e ... + sp
say what they
and ~~...~~ dislike us have seen
sh might I ... they could never
talk about ~~reality~~ captain
where you've been
I have heard how they are and I hate it)

untitled
song
for a

one day he chose
to blow nothingness
away
absence

with a breath
God made it come to be
emptied his lung
to reveal the world
we see
(mountains everything)
then he turned
away
spoken: now he cast his
glance upon us
again
will he breathe us
in again?

one day
He blew it out He exhaled
Blew nothing away
He Emptied his lung
To reveal the world today (mountains & everything)
Will he take it in?
O aye I think he will
And so doing
many living dreams will kill
he blew it out
like a candle in reverse
the dark was doused
the blow became the earth
he will take it in
every laugh & quake
breathe it in
for his own breathing's sake
and we will be
re-circulated in
~~metastasized~~ our souls absorbed
and metamorphed again
to circulate, to
breath or his urine
a poison, as sometimes
I'm sure we've been
As nourishment
For a Lord without a thought
Of all the love
&loss that she has wrought
B will he take it in
o aye I think he will
will he take it in
o aye I think he will

~~but he~~ will not get the wise
~~and there is only me~~

That's me
only one who knows
that's me
won't breathe me with his
won't breat
and I will s

he car

Noise: Silence
Diego Fonseca, *translated by* Ellen Jones

> 'It was written I should be loyal to the nightmare of my choice'
> —Joseph Conrad, *Heart of Darkness*

Every disaster has its own sound. Ask around. Before, there are the noises of everyday life—passing cars, laughter in the playground, birdsong. During, each one has its own unique soundtrack—a roar, a belligerent wind, a kind of cracking. But for a while after the event, just before a semblance of normality returns with its attendant noises, silence reigns.

Witnesses from Fukushima say that a definitive quiet settled over the air right before the tsunami that swallowed up the nuclear plant in 2011. That same silence blanketed the coast for a long while after the disaster. Chernobyl was condemned to a mortuary silence that continues to this day. Hiroshima was extinguished before any air raid sirens could go off. I myself felt a strange pause, like someone had stoppered up all the outside noise, at the Ground Zero Memorial in New York. The same sense of suspension prevails if you visit the grey stelae at the Jewish Museum in Berlin, where the silence is only broken if someone walks across the metal masks spread out along that mournful corridor.

The state of shock provoked by a crisis can manifest as hysterical screaming or weeping, but also as an inevitable, incredible, heart-breaking silence—a silence we must adopt ourselves when faced with those expressions of pain. In 2017 I returned to Mexico City ten days after the so-called Great Bitchquake from Hell. And as soon as I set foot in the street I realised the city was still on pause. The earthquake had silenced the voices of its boisterous crowds and sapped all its energy, turning that great city—the Beast—into a shy, inward-looking little animal. Quaking in its boots.

I arranged to meet some friends for dinner at a restaurant in Colonia Roma, a few streets from the ruins of Álvaro Obregón 286. We had all the right intentions: I thought that being there, confronting part of the city that had collapsed, might ward something off. Some fear, some anxiety, who knows, maybe even the silence that was making our sobs and words stick in our throats.

The conversation in the restaurant started off morosely, as though we all had the black cloud of a wake hanging over us. A communal, anonymous funeral, one where we mourned people—who some of us had seen go—as well as a collective sense of comfort, now that everything we used to know had vanished.

As our conversations went on, the spell of sadness dissipated slightly. My friends are pretty foulmouthed, and it turns out swearing is a good way of getting over your reverence for death. Bit by bit they each started lashing out at their fear, telling each other how shitscared they'd been, how fucking terrified, the horror of seeing their whole bloody lives flash before their eyes, the sheer fucking *fright* produced by that cocksucking motherfucking shitstorm of an earthquake.

But they didn't really manage to get hold of their dejection until they began talking about its sounds. I remember saying something about the silence that preceded Fukushima, and I definitely remember someone saying that here the Earth had neglected to warn us by silencing the birds and the dogs. As soon as the earthquake let loose, they said, it was accompanied by a unique soundtrack: the city roared.

The buildings were groaning and there wasn't a house that didn't look like it was about to split clean in two, Wil told me. Edurne said people were crying, panicking, wide-eyed but blind, like they couldn't see anything except the desperation hanging in the air. Camilo—Colombian through and through—cursed the motherfucking *hijueputa* planet for a whole five minutes, standing stock still in the middle of a street. And as soon as the stupid shaking had stopped, the shouts of the first volunteer rescuers began to fill the air: Juan Manuel, who'd been sent off somewhere to report on what had happened, saw desperation in the faces of survivors and a horrendous calm in those of the dead. Jacob had never seen so much solidarity rise so quickly to meet the horror of the immediate aftermath.

Alarms sounded. Despair was suffocating for some and hysterical for others. Then in the streets people raised their fists to ask for silence, of a different kind this time. Meanwhile family members, half the country in fact, began to make their voices heard on TV and social media. The government made a statement, but its voice was timid, and instead of demonstrating control and authority it uttered a guilty whisper that was drowned out by the uproar of angry citizens.

Noise and silence are interchangeable. Rescuers asked for silence with their fists held high in the air so they could listen for noises. The slightest sound might signify life; silence was a message from the dead to the living. For those who survived, on the other hand, the final silence—that of quiet reflection—would come when there were no more cries of response to be heard, no more live casualties to dig out, no more bodies to collect. That silence was a message from the living to their dead.

*

Earthquakes are natural disasters, but they are also political phenomena. We all talk about Mexico City's Great Bitchquake from Hell on the 19th September, but few people—myself included—talk about the other Great Bitchquake that hit Oaxaca on the 7th. Or about how there was yet another quake in Morelos. Or about how Chiapas was struck so badly it now looks like hell on earth. The municipality of Juchitán de Zaragoza was reduced to a mass of twisted iron, crushed tin drums, splinters of wood, debris and more debris piled up on a graveyard. Who's going to tell the seventy thousand inhabitants of Juchitán that the fucker didn't have it in for them, that early September?

Of Axochiapan, where they registered the epicentre of the earthquake that hit Mexico City on the 19th, we know little more than basic information, which is to say, we know that it was where they registered the epicentre of the earthquake that hit Mexico City. Sometimes not even that, because while Mexico's Seismological Service initially said that Axochiapan was the epicentre, the corresponding Service in the US moved it a little to the East: the epicentre of the earthquake that hit Mexico City, it said, was in San Felipe de Ayutla. It made no odds to them, even though 30,000 souls live in Axochiapan and barely 3,000 in San Felipe de Ayutla. The rest of the world couldn't care less about all those people. And so eventually the press decided it would be easier to move the cursor even further and locate the epicentre directly over the enormous colonial city of Puebla.

Things happen so quickly these days that not even a disaster entitles you to privileges. Just twelve days after the 7th September shook the south of the country like a flan, the crack running through Mexico City guaranteed that all other earthquakes would sink into slow oblivion. You had to really try—I have to really try—to remember that at the beginning of the month hundreds of thousands of Mexicans in the south of the country had their loved ones crushed, their fortunes lost, their futures flushed down the toilet. All the earth had to do was start fucking with the Beast and in no time at all the Great Bitchquake from Hell had a brand-new address and had been appropriated by the capital.

A largely poverty-stricken state in the country's south is very different to the macrocephalic capital of a nation. Mexico City is a global metropolis, just as well-known on the streets of Moscow as it is in the slums of Johannesburg. Meanwhile Oaxaca and Chiapas sound like exotic destinations for do-gooding, pro-indigenous-rights tourists from the First World. San Felipe de Ayutla could just as well be a church, to the uninformed reader. And, frankly, poor Axochiapan sounds like cough medication.

For these reasons, the Great Bitchquake from Hell will always be remembered on the 19th and not the 7th: because no matter how often Oaxaca and Chiapas and Morelos and Puebla are split apart, whether by the earth or by their own people, they're just too small compared with the Beast. There's a general distinction, *grosso modo*, drawn by the average citizen, and it has a crude brutality: Oaxaca is essentially poor, Morelos is essentially poor, while Mexico City is rich. In Puebla everyone goes to mass, while Mexico City is the playground of *mirreyes*, pampered rich kids who do Pilates. Chiapas is practically Guatemala; Mexico City is Mexico.

The earth could claim any one of us, but it kills with greater certainty when it thunders under the feet of the poor, condemning those who survive to a life of even greater destitution. Just as Chiapas signifies a life no one wants—a life of sheer misery—so too its Great Bitchquake is less Great than that of the metropolis that will claim fame and glory for as long as humans exist. Oaxaca is too far from swanky Polanco's upscale shopping centres, it takes too long to get there, there are too many dark-skinned Indians who have no Twitter presence. San Felipe de Ayutla is a sign by the side of the motorway that you'll barely even notice as you drive past at 130 kilometres an hour. But Mexico City is home to powerful people who look down on other citizens with disdain from their towers and gated communities.

Who will take responsibility for Oaxaca, Chiapas, Axochiapan and their mini bitchquakes when all the spotlights of the world focus automatically on the famous city of México-Tenochtitlán and declare theirs to be the only, the real, the famous Great Bitchquake from Hell?

I'm as guilty of this as any. I heard instantly of Mexico City's earthquake. The ones in Oaxaca and Chiapas I only learned about by accident. I hadn't a fucking clue what San Felipe de Ayutla was until *San Google* told me.

*

I'd arrived in the city two days before that dinner with friends, and I noticed that in the streets of the historic centre, in Santa Fe, Condesa, Polanco, in the south, near Tlalpan, in my old neighbourhood Cuauhtémoc, the city was encased in a strange bubble. Maybe it was just me, but there were no car horns debating traffic rules, no transport police exacerbating the city's chaos with their whistles. The amateur guitarists had disappeared from restaurants. I didn't see a single one of those unbearable organ grinders dressed in zoo-keepers' uniforms. All the romantic ballad singers had vanished. I didn't once hear the cry of the gaaaaaaaaaaas man, nor the girl buying *colchones tambores refrigeradores estufas lavadoras microondas o algo de fierro viejo que venda*. How do you silence a city whose very fabric is woven to make noise?

*

Mexico sits on some pretty wild territory. All down the country's ribs and flanks there runs a fault, and under the capital stretches a sort of cut or wound or gash, and a drained lake the texture of melting ice. There's a lethal desert in the north and a necklace of volcanoes to the east capable of vomiting the planet's guts up when you least expect it, onto cities populated by millions. And even so, there seems to be something innate about humans' desire to defy the impossible.

Neither the sun nor death can be looked at steadily, wrote La Rochefoucauld. But I reckon the people living in this mess of a city—of a country?—have had to face up, thirty-three years to the day after the last major earthquake, to the reality that they've chosen to live on top of death itself. Any day now, at any moment, the Earth might rear up, because apparently, it's time, and then half of Mexico will be trapped in the bubble of silence that precedes and follows an earthquake.

And yet, nobody really moves away. It's not like there's been a mass migration, people displacing themselves in their millions. And this isn't exclusive to Mexico. People will always return to places where nature keeps reminding them they're not welcome. Vesuvius is still surrounded by grumbling Italians. If the Big One ever hits California, where the convergence of multiple faults creates enormous subterranean pressure, thirty million people and a big slice of the United States will end up under the Pacific.

There's a kind of angry resignation or obstinacy in someone who accepts their lot and lives in nature's thrall, when all that can be done is trust their luck will hold. The earth will inevitably quake again and if you don't have decent engineers to construct the floor under your feet, you'll end up as fertilizer unless you move. And people don't move—we don't move. People curse the ground and stare at it, their faces sad, and surrender, once again, to an existential silence where questions like who am I and why did I come will sustain them until the real one, the big one hits.

*

In *Et la vie continue*, Kiarostami drives a tired old man to his villa in a clapped-out car. The man is dressed in a threadbare suit, perhaps the only one he possesses, and he wears it elegantly. When they arrive, Kiarostami asks the old man if his son can have a drink of water. The villa is nothing more than the ruins of a once-habitable farmhouse somewhere in Iran. An earthquake has levelled all the houses made of sandy adobe. What's left of them are a few half-walls with bricks poking out of them like twisted teeth and roofs so ragged they look like they've been clawed at by a furious god.

The old man doesn't live in the better house—which is still a dump except it's got a terrace—but in a two-storey structure so bare that it looks like it simply emerged from the barren dust, like the earthquake didn't actually destroy anything, just reclaimed what already belonged to the earth.

There is fertile land a bit further on and perhaps even some patches of sandy ground, if he wanted it, a couple of miles uphill, but the old man inherited this house and in this house he will stay. He won't leave the ruin that is his home, nor the ground that shakes it. He is *from* there. Through everything, despite everything, and against everything, he *belongs* there. To that ground, to the silence encircling him and the sounds that break the silence.

I thought about that man when I saw the inhabitants of Mexico City sweeping the pavements outside their houses or arranging the chairs in their living rooms in preparation for another morning, a few days after the earthquake. Why do people who live in the Beast decide to stay in the Beast? Why do people living in flats so fragile they may as well be made of glass go back inside, encase themselves in those walls, and wait until—today, tomorrow, thirty-three years from now—the ceilings and the skies above cave in?

I know there are some who are unable to leave, but I also suspect there are many more who choose to stay. Some are more scared of their mortgage than they are of an earthquake. But others seem to deliberately stare down the forces of nature and the Fates. Where before they might have felt a desire to stay, now they will feel angry. Where before it was a choice, perhaps now determination is taking over. This is no heroism. Stubbornness, perhaps.

They will all experience that silence each time the Earth—which in this part of the world means the back of a brutish, feral animal—decides to buck. The floors will split in two, they will despair—and they will return to clear away the dust, straighten the pictures on the walls, pick the chairs up off the floors and wait for the next paroxysm from the bowels of the earth. *Amor fati*.

*

During that dinner with Wil, Camilo, Edurne, Juan Manuel and Jacob, ten days after the Great Bitchquake from Hell, the wine and mezcal began to loosen our tongues. We raised our voices a little despite the quiet in the streets, where even the cars were whispering. Talking saves lives.

Only once during our conversation—it must have been around midnight—was the litany of voices broken. A boy came by selling sweets and cigarettes with his mother: one or other of them cracked a joke, but it was the boy—four, five, seven years old—who cut through the thin air we breathed with a burst of laughter. Short, high, crystalline: alive. It probably sounds trite to make innocence and obliviousness the cure for that silent fear of what-might-happen. But it's just possible that it's those two things that keep convincing millions of people to build their homes—and their lives—on the fragile back of a nation.

This morning I woke up with a quick laugh like the sun

Hao Guang Tse (謝皓光)

my very very clean

hands, my nails bitten

in orderly fashion—

white moon at base
of the nail,
lunula?

I'm closely
aligned to laughter &

at three removes
from the moon— sun

simply is a close
up star,

shows up dust
in corners, dust
simply is close
up skin. I'm at

a hundred removes from
dust, & fully aligned

to skin

Edgelords
Geoffrey Mak

'Will not a tiny speck very close to our vision blot out the glory of the world, and leave only a margin by which we see the blot? I know no speck so troublesome as self.'
—George Eliot, *Middlemarch*

1.

Why must Cordelia die? I've asked this question to a number of people a number of times, except the answer was always wrong because the question is based on a misreading of *King Lear*. For the longest time, I thought Lear was the one who killed Cordelia before dragging his daughter's dead body on stage, meaning *Lear* wouldn't technically be a tragedy, in the Aristotelian sense, since Lear's madness would introduce a random act of violence. For years, I took this as a model for morality: there is good and there is evil, and then there's madness. You can't stop madness. You can lock yourself up twelve stories high in some corner of New York, but that particular train is still coming. It will plow through the Hudson River, emerge from the pavement down Manhattan on Broadway, right up to your building, pummel up the elevator shaft and straight through your door, and it will run you over. Because madness doesn't follow the rules. It isn't afraid of you. Which is why it's so terrifying when, in the play's final scene, the Duke of Kent stands over a bloodbath of the English monarchy, and asks, *Is this the promised end?* Except I got the part wrong about how it actually ends. Doesn't matter. Cordelia dies anyway.

Over the years, this would serve as a cautionary tale, a kind of bad omen, for dark times and inconvenient revelations, during which I waded through the unsorted phenomena of lived experience, attempting, but failing, to cull the appropriate narratives out of nonsense, glean the cause and effect, locate the tragic flaw. The period I'm writing about would start during the Obama years, and transition into the apocalyptic logic of the Trump presidency. During those years, I worked in New York advertising for the former Design Director at *Interview*, the former editor of *The New York Observer*, and one of the first hundred employees at Google. On an irregular basis, I wrote art reviews for magazines, talked shit, showed face at gallery openings and warehouse parties when my friends were DJ'ing, and I never asked for list. I read everything I could find, opened myself up to the contagion of the world, made note of who had the fewest lines of dialogue in *The Great Gatsby* (those with the most power and those with the least), and precisely at which point Proust turns on the Duchesse de Guermantes (when she declares, at her salon, that she doesn't care for contemporary painting). I maintained the ability to, on command, recite the Clinton administration's policy in Yugoslavia, or state the reasons why an American intervention in Syria may or may not have prevented ISIS, which is to say I kept up with the news. And when I could not keep up with history, history caught up with me. I'd been reading on my parents' balcony in California when I got the text from my editor at the conservative magazine

I wrote for, alerting me that our login credentials got phished by the Syrian Electronic Army. A week later, when the magazine interviewed the SEA about the data breach, the hacker collective responded curtly, "It was a joke."

Except nothing was funny, because nothing made sense to me—I either got the timing wrong, waited too long, or misunderstood the premise to such an extent that I started working from structures in my mind completely divorced from whatever I could confirm in the people around me.

These years I travelled frequently. I lived in Istanbul and then in New York, spent time in Hong Kong, Paris, and travelled through former Yugoslavia. In Northern Iraq, I accidentally took photos inside a Yazidi temple where no photos were allowed, only to read seven years later that the temple had likely been destroyed by ISIS. Another weekend, I flew into New York from Berlin, went to a warehouse party in Brooklyn until ten in the morning, crashed on a friend's couch, then emerged six hours later to moderate a panel with the Goethe-Institute on international queer literature. The week I sold my own international queer novel, I went to Dover Street Market, bought a Rick Owens trench coat off the runway, rode the elevator down to the ground floor bar and ordered myself a glass of cava (which is to say that sometimes, things were so good I thought my life, like the times, could only get better).

This was during the years I divided between New York and Berlin. That I never really knew where I was living contributed to my recurring cycles of disorientation. I had a habit of starting my life, and then restarting it up again every few months, as if passing through unrelated episodes I didn't always finish before moving onto the next. One month, I rented a studio on Maybachufer across the canal from the luxury residences on Paul-Linke Ufer, and by the next, I was living in a narrow room in Mitte with a single window that opened onto dumpsters in the courtyard from which, some sweaty Monday mornings after coming back from the club, the smell of damp socks and garlic would waft into the room where, passed out from ketamine, I dreamt of becoming famous.

I finished my novel in an apartment with a view overlooking Görlitzer Park. I didn't celebrate, nor did I do very much on my birthdays, as they were private landmarks I'd acknowledge privately. In Berlin, I found I was often alone, and then suddenly surrounded by three thousand at once, at a club or a Biennial exhibition or a street protest in Friedrichshain. Once, I wore Rick Owens sneakers to a housing protest where demonstrators in black balaclavas hurled stun grenades over the crowd and onto a fortress of ballistic shields: an image that accurately represents the delusions I had about Berlin and whatever I was supposed to be doing at this point in my life.

In an apartment by the canal, I read the transcript from the Supreme Court ruling that legalized gay marriage in all fifty states, and on the night that forty-nine were shot dead at the Pulse nightclub in Miami, I was at Berghain. The morning I found out that Alton Sterling and Philando Castile were shot unarmed by racist cops, I was acting on the set for a web series alongside a German philosopher, a male model, two Syrian refugees, and a hedge fund analyst. That the series was titled *DISCREET: An Intelligence Agency for the*

People might suggest that I was at least in on the joke, except I was not.

I never was, I kept failing to see the punch line. As it happened, I would fail to get the bigger picture for a pretty long time before things got weird, before the part in the song where "*Sounds make you cry / Some nights you dance with tears in your eyes.*" Around the same time, I remember reading DeLillo's story "The Itch" about the character who "heard what sounded like words as his urine hit the water," because during the year that story came out, so did I. Loud noises would begin to disturb me. I would make excuses to stay inside. At the time, I had been house-sitting a friend's top-floor apartment in Prenzlauer Berg, across from a massive crane that, during thunderstorms, I imagined would swing in my direction and crash straight into the sliding glass doors of the balcony.

Those days, all that could hold my attention were reports of the Ergenekon Trials, and the wisdom of crowds. Outside, I made labyrinthine walks around my neighborhood, taking fast turns from the Turkish food stands and into the discount supermarket, keeping note of who walked into both places after me and didn't buy a thing. "How old are you? What year is this?" a police officer would one day ask me over the phone, after a botched ayahuasca ceremony in Brandenburg, during which I climbed out of a window on the second floor and jumped, convinced I was being held against my will by a religious cult, only to run out into miles of open grain fields with no cars in sight. Months later, I would find those questions useful to ask myself on a regular basis. I began forgetting what year this was and where I had come from, around the time I found myself at Berghain one early Monday morning, sobbing so uncontrollably on the dance floor that the DJ (it was Efdemin) stopped the music and put on "Journey in Satchidananda," suggesting that it might be time for some people to go home.

The truth is that I was a long way from home. I was on the verge of a mental breakdown. Here's a cut to just a few months later, August 2018:

This is a 30-year-old male admitted to Parkside West on a 5150 hold for danger to self… This patient reports that he attempted to overdose due to severe auditory hallucinations. They are causing him distress. They are causing him to feel hopeless and helpless and causing him to continue to feel suicidal, depressed, and wanting to end his life so he does not have to hear the voices anymore… He was also restless and wanted to be left alone, and minimized his problems. He was given Zyprexa 10mg twice a day… was found to be positive for multiple substances including ketamine and amphetamines. His mood is irritable. His affect is constricted. His speech is with an irritable tone. He admits to suicidal ideation. He denies any homicidal ideations. He admits to severe auditory hallucinations. He has severe paranoia… He continues to feel overwhelmed and hopeless that he will get any better.

This is an excerpt from my psychiatric report, compiled shortly after I boarded a next-day flight from Berlin to California, and committed myself to the inpatient psychiatric clinic at the Citrus Valley Medical Center less than two weeks after I turned thirty. Only at my most dissociative am I inclined to see this as a literary metaphor for the dissolution of the times, but I don't make those connections anymore. My twenties were already over before I could make good on any possible warnings, and by then, it didn't matter. The train came for me anyway.

2.

Here is a transcript from C-SPAN that provides a sense of what, maybe just ten years ago, would have been considered paranoid, yet in 2018 was a paragon of being informed:

> SENATOR DICK DURBIN: I said to Senator Cornyn, my friend, when he said he thought consumers were aware that information is gathered on them… I said I'm sure he's wrong. We have now put a little piece of electric tape over the camera on my laptop.
> CHRISTOPHER WYLIE: Good.
> SENATOR DICK DURBIN: Most people do, now. Because they're being watched and they might not even know it.

This is from the testimony of twenty-eight-year-old whistleblower Christopher Wylie, former Research Director at Cambridge Analytica before the UK Senate Judiciary Committee. Wylie, self-identified as a "gay Canadian vegan," recounted before the Senate how Cambridge Analytica harvested over fifty million Facebook profiles for the Trump campaign in the US and the Brexit campaign in the UK. Dubbed by Wylie as a "full-service propaganda machine," Cambridge Analytica employed personality quizzes that harvested psychographic data to target political ads specializing in "disinformation," "rumors," and "Kompromat"—a "military-style operation" in what was referred to internally as "Big Daddy."

I followed this story as it developed in the *Guardian* and the *Times*, watched Wylie testify before Parliament on C-SPAN for four hours, and then again before the US Senate for three hours and forty minutes. So preoccupied was I with stories about cultural conditioning, manufactured consent, and disinformation campaigns happening across social platforms that enacted a system of classically conditioned propaganda on a global scale. I learned, for instance, that as early as 2014, Cambridge Analytica began using Facebook data to test responses to images of people scaling walls, and slogans like "The NSA is watching you" or "Build The Wall" or "Drain The Swamp," two years before Donald Trump hired the firm and began parroting those same slogans across social platforms. Wylie describes the work of Cambridge Analytica as designed to trigger "some of the worst characteristics in people, such as neuroticism, paranoia, and racial biases," otherwise traits that might describe the defining cultural characteristics of these years I'm writing about.

When asked by Senator Cory Booker why Cambridge Analytica was allegedly focused on "suppressing African American voters," Wylie responded, "You'll have to ask Mr. Bannon," who was then the VP of Cambridge Analytica and executive chairman of the conservative network *Breitbart News,* before he became CEO of the Trump campaign. Reportedly, Bannon charted systematized "voter disengagement tactics" that targeted black users with divisive content that, in one example, reminded them about Hillary Clinton's 1990s description of black youths as "super predators" in an effort to discourage black support for Clinton. (Coincidentally or not, black voter turnout for a presidential election declined in 2016 for the first time in twenty years.)

Here you see the idea that if you control the narrative, you have the keys to the culture. "Given the influence that story has on our everyday lives, and that popular culture is barraging us with story on a regular basis, we must remain ever vigilant as to the messaging in those stories," wrote one writer in *Breitbart.* It was an elaboration on what's known as the Breitbart Doctrine—"Politics is downstream from culture"—of which Bannon was an exemplary follower. Part sales pitch, part American lyric, the line had served as the founding principle of *Breitbart News* when Andrew Breitbart first launched the site in 2007 in efforts to reroute the cultural narratives for a far-right audience.

I had never heard of Breitbart, not really, until the rise of one of its senior editors Milo Yiannopoulos, an English conservative and self-described "dangerous faggot" who became the emergent poster child of what became known as the alt-right. Curdling around online forums such as Reddit and 4Chan, this cesspool of neoreactionary anti-feminists and white supremacists who made up the alt-right would become a particular focal point for Bannon when he headed the Trump campaign.

"The alt-right is the new left," declared white supremacist Richard Spencer, who coined the term, since "we're the ones thinking the unthinkable," which now included some of Spencer's new ideas such as "peaceful ethnic cleansing." Yiannopoulos would also describe the alt-right as "the new punk," because they were "transgressive, subversive, fun." Here, you find an adaptation of Pat Buchanan's declared "religious war" over "the soul of America" at the 1992 RNC, readapted for a digital generation credited with codifying "trolling" into the culture as a legitimate political strategy.

In a video from 2017, Yiannopoulos is shown singing "America the Beautiful" to Richard Spencer and giving him a *Sieg Heil* salute, another "unthinkable" that would be interpreted as ironic because of all that transgressive and subversive fun they were having. Yet it would not be considered ironic when, in another leaked video, Nigel Oakes, founder of Cambridge Analytica's parent company SCL, stated about Hitler: "He didn't have a problem with the Jews at all, but people didn't like the Jews, so he just leveraged an artificial enemy. Well that's exactly what Trump did, he leveraged the Muslims. That's what Trump did—he had the balls to say what people wanted to hear."

*

Below is a framed poem hung above the urinal at Café Loup in New York, which served for me both as a nostalgic token, like the restaurant itself, from a bygone era, as well as a warning, ignored, in dark times ahead:

WOLF CREDO
Respect the elders
Teach the young
Cooperate with the pack

Play when you can
Hunt when you must
Rest in between

Share your affections
Voice your feelings
Leave your mark.

In the thirty seconds it took to piss, my eyes would zero in on the words "the pack"—conjuring the image of sex cults, mass suicides, charismatic leaders who lured people into orgies, or Ponzi schemes, with telegenic smiles and promises of belonging. I wondered when, exactly, "community" passes into "groupthink," when the mere "collective" becomes "mob mentality." Such was evidently the case when a news story known as "Gamergate" came out about hackers, organized on 4Chan, who made death threats and rape threats to several feminist bloggers in what would become a years-long doxxing and harassment campaign of leaking contact details and personal information with threats like "I'll rape you and put your head on a stick" and "Tits or get the fuck out."

Petra Davis reported finding a website that advertise sex services with her address and images of mutilated women on the front page, under the tagline "Fuck her till she screams, filth whore, rape me all night cut me open." Revenge porn with Zoe Quinn was sent to her family and employers. A video game of Anita Sarkeesian was created and distributed where users could punch her face until it was blue and swollen. And Kathy Sierra received photoshopped images of her face with a noose next to her head, a shooting target pointed at her face, and her head being gagged in underwear.

Here was an example of the pack gone astray, who no longer distinguished between hunt and play. By then, my worldview had corroded so deeply into the morbid that I assumed, at all times, that somebody, some group or other, was out to get me. I was never safe. *Someone* was always watching. More and more, people I knew started recommending I get on encrypted messaging apps like Signal, or the internet browser Tor, and I took their advice. I didn't know what anyone might want by spying on me, but I assumed it could and would be used against me the day the Feds came knocking.

One afternoon, late summer, I was having coffee in the garden of the Standard Hotel when a friend told me he'd been contacted, for a job interview, by someone at the CIA. I said, "I'll never know if you get the job, because if you do, you won't be allowed to tell me." He replied that he may not be able to tell me, but if I see him one day wearing an expensive coat, I'll know why. We laughed like cavaliers, because the sun was bright, and it was still 2014, which is to say early, before the paranoia set in, and we were able to joke about things that seemed to belong to a remote reality.

Some months later, I saw him walk into a mutual friend's gallery opening wearing a three-quarter-length leather coat. Spotting me across the room, he came over and whispered in my ear, "I got the coat," to my giddy delight.

Whether or not this is just an eccentric anecdote along a string of unrelated events, I don't know. After that, we carried on our civilian lives. I continued to see him at parties and openings, and eventually I stopped thinking about the conversation we had at the Standard Hotel. This would be another story that I did not stick around long enough to find out the ending. After a certain point, it stopped seeming remarkable during a time defined by questions about whether or not a cell phone tower was in fact a cell phone tower, or an "active GSM base station" designed to intercept cell phone data operated remotely by the NSA. My preoccupation with these stories was my idea of "being informed." Every threat was to be taken seriously: the promise of the wall, or the boogeyman under the bed, or behind the camera, staring back from the top of the laptop screen.

3.

In 2015, I attended Art Basel Miami Beach, an annual event held at the Miami Beach Convention Center in December during which multiple commodities are available for sale or as trade collateral: paintings, new media, cultural capital, thumb drives, Foursquare check-ins, smartphone videos of the semi-nude, a critique on the collapse of the social contract, TASCHEN monographs, and glitter.

This makes Art Basel difficult to criticize because it seldom pretends to be anything other than what it is. Its absence of pretence has made talking about the fair avoided altogether, taboo because it is "degrading for art and artists," as Christian Viveros-Fauné described in *Artnet*, or what Aly Weisman stated in *Business Insider* "has become as much about the parties as the art." You might ask when exactly the "has become" took place, when exactly Art Basel had been "about the art," as if its decision thirteen years ago to base the Swiss art-fair franchise in a city with a twenty-four hour party district, proximity to the US cocaine trade, and the 0% tax on sales and income were quirky atmospherics, the local color. Hans Ulrich Obrist, who mentored the fair's director Noah Horrowitz as an associate at London's Serpentine Galleries, himself confessed to having "little knowledge of, or interest, in art fairs."

On parties, Barbara Gladstone of Gladstone Gallery stated to the *New York Times*, "There are too many of them and I don't think it's that useful." Useful to what? The answer came more directly from Luhring Augustine of the Luhring Augustine Gallery. "There are a lot of people who come for the parties—there are people who don't even come to the fair," he said. "But we do business here."

Business as usual was the main factor in navigating the fairgrounds. Upon entering the convention center, one encounters the so-called Circle of Power: Gagosian, Zwirner, Rosen, Hauser & Wirth, Cooper, et al. The opportunity for discovery, i.e. the 90% of the fair beyond the Kusamas, the Christopher Wools, the Krugers, the Frankenthalers, should have been an exciting prospect but was, in practice, deflating. In *Artnet*, Kenny Schachter hyperbolically described the fair as "the end of art history," a Fukuyama-like prophecy that might explain rather than contradict why the fair felt the need, since 2014, to introduce the "Survey" section to "present precise art historical projects," tucked neatly alongside of the fair's main action. The main action was, you could say, the bigger history lesson at large: that the fair was not the end of art history, nor was it at all an anomaly in the history of art, or of its sales, dating back to the festivals of the late Middle Ages during which guild masters and apprentices set up "booths" that exhibited crafts for public evaluation, for public sales. The art history lesson here was the discrepancy between what we like to consider as the artworld and what it actually is. Or rather, what it had always been.

Somehow, the fair managed to piss everyone off, from its main players who were hasty to disavow emotional investments in their financial calculations, to regular fairgoers, comparing email invites and Instagram stories #aboutlast-night, who were at the fair to complain how they wanted to be somewhere else.

The tension and anxiety reached an alarming pitch when twenty-four-year old Siyuan Zhao of New York stabbed a thirty-three-year-old stranger in the neck with an X-Acto knife, just outside the Freedman Fitzpatrick Gallery booth. When interrogated by the officers about the crime, Zhao stated, "I had to kill her and two more!" and "I had to watch her bleed!"

Miami Herald photographer Rudy Perez was on the scene ready to shoot photos that would be introduced online with trigger warnings for "graphic content." *The Gothamist*, *CNN*, *FoxNews*, and *The Huffington Post* each picked up the story, leading not with the stabbing itself but that "witnesses thought it was art."

Assuming for the first initial seconds that the stabbing was "performance art" with "fake blood" would not be considered abnormal, in light of how certain concertgoers at the Bataclan Concert Hall during the Paris attacks thought the first gunshots fired were part of the music. Part of the art. It seemed reasonable enough after witnessing the stabbing, a traumatic event in its own right, except that was not the story the press was interested in. Gregg Hill, a witness who stated, "I never would have thought there would be a stabbing at Art Basel" was described by *Paper Mag* as a character out of an *Onion* piece. Something ridiculous. A satire. A salacious event at an elitist art fair that continues to mine the deepest social insecurities of this nation's liberal intelligentsia on a yearly basis.

The victim was wheeled away by paramedics to Jackson Memorial. Zhao was arrested on an attempted murder charge. The blood was quickly removed. The fair went on as planned. Click. Shoot. Cut. Send.

*

For those of us who were not doing business here, most of the daytime was spent coked out and sleep deprived, wandering up and down Miami Beach with press pins and stickers, hunting for the VIP lounge in rain boots and Doc Martens.

I was here because after plans to spend New Years in Berlin had failed to materialize, I decided to reallocate the budget to getting fashionably plastered in South Beach, Miami. That weekend, the city had flooded. It came late on Thursday night as a sort of Biblical cleanse once the business at the temple of art was done, and the fair was open to the plebian middle class. That night, those who may or may not have flown in on delayed flights from New York shuttled back and forth between New York parties transplanted and reinvented in Miami: Horse Meat Disco, Topical Cream, Mixpack, Bunker, GHE20G0TH1K. Text messages were sent, asking if the nebulous *there* was better than the permanently uninteresting *here*. "I think we're gonna go to NADAWAVE," said one. "When does Objekt go on?" "Is Perez the same thing PAMM?" Paris Hilton or Alicia Keys may or may not have been playing a party in Wynwood. It may or may not have been worth the price of a taxi.

After two parties and sixty dollars worth of taxis up and down Collins Avenue, I'd ended up at party to see Julianna Huxtable and Venus X at Kill Your Idol. The bar was packed. Somebody reported seeing Jacolby Satterwhite and M.I.A. there, when in fact Jacolby Satterwhite, who was exhibiting a piece and hosting a party, was allegedly not in Miami. Dev Hynes, after a performance at PAMM that one attendee had described as "just okay," was now waiting in line for the gender-neutral bathrooms. I was also in line waiting for a gender-neutral bathroom when a girl leaned over and asked, "Do you know where I can find any coke?"

I did not. Landing in the middle of Miami and finding a coke dealer off the street didn't seem like the smartest thing to do. Others got more creative. One person I knew had stored two grams of coke in a nasal spray bottle and carried it on the plane, while another packed pills and mixed them in with a bottle of Melatonin. Another had stored small bags in a Soylent pouch packed sideways in his carryon to dodge the X-rays. "The powder blends in with the powder, the plastic blends in with the plastic," as he described it.

Back on the dance floor, a friend said, "There's Ryder Ripps behind me looking like a fuckboy."

"Wait, I don't know what he looks like," I said.

"He looks like a fuckboy."

I wedged my way through the dance floor, wearing a white turtleneck and the straps of my BAGGU backpack crossed over my chest like a harness. Across from me, the girl who asked for coke was now dancing on the couch beside her friend with bleached blonde hair, swinging his shirt over his head like a lasso. It was New York but not—the "but not" being the crucial factor in everyone letting their pants down, the "but not" factor of senior trips and study abroad programs, weekends in Palms Springs and Sunday nights at Berghain.

Even the word Basel had become a code word for cultural excess, an adlib to fill in the "What happens at stays at" dictum, a pride festival for Northeast liberals, an excuse to use "art" as stand-ins for "social awareness" and "criticality" that, instead of reining in excess, otherwise affirms the 24-hour hedonism of coke and neon. If politics is downstream from culture, then here was the culture: cultish, narcissistic, obsessed with petty optics over a coherent ideology, and eternally paranoid about minor distinctions up and down the social caste system. For that week, and that week only, South Beach would become a hall of mirrors for New York galleries, New York DJs, serving as the third leg in the revolving door of the East Coast underground, in and out of Bushwick, in and out of Boston, people I recognized but knew nothing about except that they had enough money to spend a weekend in Miami: the supposedly fun thing we would never do again unless everyone else was also down there with us pretending to look at art.

4.

Another snapshot of the culture in excess: one weekend, in Berlin, I was at a monthly party called Herrensauna at the Bertrams club on Maybachufer. It was run by a former bartender at Berghain who went by Herrenscheide, German for "male cunt." The party's target clientele were unofficially described as "gay skinheads," according to a friend who described the party to me as "half fashion, half gay sex." I arrived that morning at six, hiding inside my sock what I thought was a gram of speed, but was actually a gram of meth, bought for seven euro at the last party I was at as "special speed" from a friend I knew who owed me a favor.

The party itself was a fashionable simulacrum with no original, itself a reference to the Fall 2015 show for the fashion label Vetements, which was staged inside a gay sex club with Shifted's "Chapter 69" as the soundtrack, yet another reference towards the gay sex that actually *was* happening at Herrensauna, which had booked Shifted to play the headlining slot that morning of the party, and hired a model as the bouncer who actually did walk the Vetements shows in Paris.

Everything was a reference, a sign. At the party, we were not so much socializing as we were performing types, which often confounded me. I was never sure which side of the counterculture I was expected to perform: art critic, ad man from New York, technogoth turning looks at the club, or a foot fetishist with a kink for golden showers. I just knew that once I located my role, my "character," it was important to deviate as little as possible.

On my way in, I ran into a rapper who went by Palm Trees and performed under the name VIOLENCE, and we started talking Cormac McCarthy. I saw another friend from New York, a photographer, who was wearing a white lace Craig Green top he got at an employee discount at Opening Ceremony. I saw a sizeable amount of "skinheads," both in person and on Instagram posts from the party, insofar as they might be personally anti-fascist, yet were visibly channelling all the hallmarks of skinhead regalia: black Doc Martens with white laces, tattoos of dogs and Greek statues, Fred Perry polos and suspenders, replete with the party's wrist-stamp showing the letter H inside a laurel crown. This was an archetype—a "character"—I occasionally saw around Berlin, on the U-Bahn, or smoking outside the späti. Multiple times, I saw men with tattoos of the Chanel logo, on the inside of someone's forearm or behind his neck—a symbol that might appear curious coming from a luxury womenswear brand, were it not, as I learned later, an oblique reference to Coco Chanel's career as a covert intelligence officer for the Nazis during the German occupation.

If I didn't know any better, I might've called this… *the new punk?* Fascinating Fascism or Fashion Fascists, either way, it depended on your understanding of "the new," what with the party's use of anti-gay skinhead symbols reappropriated as gay sexual fetish, following a tradition of transgressive artists from Genet to Siouxsie Sioux to Gabber Eleganza. There was no observable compass to be found here, preferable to a generation that adopted a shock-and-confuse strategy towards any attempts by the outsider media to make sense of the culture. Here, entire histories with contingent localities got recycled and posted on social media for the shocks and the lulz. Conveniently dropped were the working class values integral to British skinhead culture in the seventies, perhaps its only salvageable detail. Instead, the party deployed "the look" indiscriminately in circles of streetwear bloggers and runways in Paris, effectively obscuring any of its political coordinates by the absence of a moral compass.

I wondered when and where this mattered and when and where it didn't. Down in the basement, the dance floor was filled with shirtless muscle queens and a drug dealer I knew, fully-clothed, working the floor. When the photographer and I needed a light, we tried to strike a lighter, but it wouldn't light, because there wasn't enough oxygen in the air.

Legitimately, this party was an operable men's sauna: heat, fog, gay sex. Lines of speed started clumping up once you tapped it out onto your smartphone, though people were mostly taking milliliters of GBL, rationed off in the privacy of the dark rooms furnished with ripped up couches and a leather sling. I was off on the dance floor dancing like an overheating robot because I was on speed that was actually meth, and I was trying to find a place to park myself until I could ride out my assigned role for the night: the dumb American who took too much.

We were all too much. In the words of trend forecasting agencies, our roles were "influencers," which implied an elusive "audience" we all knew didn't refer to each other exactly, but someone out there watching, on Facebook or the livestream, otherwise followers in the reality TV show that was our youth culture in real time. Here was the manifestation of a generation spawned by the millennial emergence of a global elite, depicted on social as eternal leisure—an essentially groundless fantasy enacted entirely on EasyJet miles and corporate-sponsored afterparties. That our theater of excess might be alienating to "someone out there" was not a question on anyone's mind, because no one ever asked who it was we were supposed to be "influencing," who those people might be; because it would be poor taste to wonder what they might want from us as they scrolled through our social feeds, and whether or not their feelings towards us might be less than purely aspirational.

5.

If politics is downstream from culture, it's because the culture makes no fucking sense. For instance, take this story I heard about Kanye West that I often told people in certain media circles, about someone who worked for Kanye on a video shoot. Before Kanye arrives on set, one of his representatives comes out to meet with the agency. She tells them, "There's something really important about Kanye that I need you to know. This might sound crazy to some of you, but Kanye does believe he's a prophet. Don't question it, and don't bring it up in front of him. This is very important. Don't tell him what to do. Do not look at him in the eye when talking. Do not ask him any direct questions. Try to treat him the way you would any other prophet." So when Kanye actually arrives, nobody looks him in the eye and nobody asks any questions. Here, the personality disorders of the prophet merge with those of a dictator: moral indignation, claims of direct access to the divine, consolidation of an "inner circle," positive perception of self paired with negative perception of the future. Everything Kanye touches here, every comment, every idea he expresses out loud turns to gold. Whenever he says something, or so much as stares at the mood board for longer than seconds, the team quarantines it off as "interesting." Valuable. This goes on for a while, because everything Kanye finds interesting, they produce. Should Kanye not like what they produce, the team starts over. Should one of Kanye's trusted advisors comment that what they produce "looks weird," the team starts over. This happens several times with two full-length videos scrapped. On the third shoot, Kanye walks past one of the interns on a couch watching a YouTube video on an iPad. Kanye is stunned. "What are you watching?" Kanye asks. The intern answers. "What do you think of it? Are you into it? Why?" After a few more lines of dialogue, Kanye receives a signal from above. He turns to the rest of the team and tells them he has an announcement: everyone must stop what they're doing and listen to this intern. He will now become the creative director of the video.

If I had ever known which video it was, I forgot, because the story itself had already become for me a contemporary parable about a culture industry based entirely upon a model of psychosis. In fact, almost ten years after I first heard the story about Kanye, I saw the same friend who told it to me, and I asked her to tell the story again. It turned out to be not at all the way I remembered it, but by then, it didn't really matter. Are you starting to see a pattern?

6.

Certain images, certain icons, became for me indicative of these years—images that don't mean anything in most contexts, but are resonant in my mind like the branded mark of a sex cult insignia. One of them: the image of a clenched fist. I saw it first, during the 2009 UC fee hike protests, and I saw it again, on TV, at the barricades in Gezi, or the squares in Kiev. Incidentally, it had also been the symbol used in the Otpor! protests in Serbia "as the brand of a bloodless revolution," recalls Srđa Popović, one of the leaders of the student-led revolution that deposed Slobodan Milošević from autocratic rule in 2000.

This is from an interview featured in the art exhibition *Seductive Exacting Realism* at Documenta14 by artist Irena Haiduk. In it, Haiduk elaborates on the work of the Centre for Applied Nonviolent Action and Strategies (CANVAS), a political NGO founded by Popović that (as revealed by Wikileaks) collaborates with US intelligence firms and think tanks to provide political consulting to pro-democracy protest movements worldwide. Since its conception in 2004, CANVAS has trained groups in over fifty countries, often covertly, years before any of the movements start making global headlines. For instance, when protesters in Tunisia deposed president Ben Ali from power in 2011, igniting the Arab Spring, CANVAS had been active in training grassroots organizations in the country since 2007. Because CANVAS's involvement is discrete, it is impossible for outside observers to discern whether or not they have been active in any given protest movement on the televised news. In the centerpiece of the exhibition, Haiduk interviews the CANVAS founder:

> HAIDUK: I can never tell when I am watching the news whether you are involved or not.
>
> POPOVIĆ: That's good. It keeps us safe. Most of the time, you will never know. If and when we do sign our work, it is after the fact. It's too dangerous in the process.

I, too, would not be able to tell. In my memory and in the news, I began looking for the tell-tale signs, which I hoped would reveal themselves back to me as details that would light up, betray the hand of their makers, like coded hand signs. I had a habit of drawing connections that could not be proven valid, but not exactly be disproven, nestled somewhere in between the "may or may not." I found similarities across disparate movements that might trace back to similar sources. For instance, I discovered that in training manuals distributed to activists, CANVAS compiled an extensive list of common non-violent strategies. The guidelines include:

- Organize blockades of highways in order to debilitate the economy and show the regime the people's power.
- Occupy key public buildings and occasional nonviolent invasions of said buildings.
- Move bulldozers in line with police barricades.

I thought of the Çarşı bulldozer in the barricades at Istanbul. Waste trucks dumping manure in the streets of Paris. The highway shutdown in Atlanta after the shooting of Philando Castille. I don't know, in each particular instance, which came first, the action observed or the prescription, or the extent to which any demonstration could be considered original. Maybe *original* isn't even relevant in this context; every protest is a copy of a copy. Maybe it didn't matter whether what feels organic actually is, or if it was orchestrated upstream by some pretty big players in the game. The difference between a staged revolution and a real one is that there is no difference. The result is the same: the regime comes down. "Assad, Chavez, Erdoğan, and Putin fear us," states Popović about CANVAS. "In Saudi Arabia, we're branded as terrorists. And when Chinese TV blames us for Hong Kong riots, it feels good. When you're banned, you attract a certain type of people. It's like a call."

Whether or not this yields to a greater story, or if these are just more questions that lead to more questions—I don't claim to know how any of this works. In years since, I only knew more and more people who felt the need to get out of bed and shut down a freeway. People active in Oakland, Zucotti Park, Gezi, Berlin, each protest seeming to pour its energies into each successive movement, increasingly stronger than the last. There was a time when all I heard was talk about eating the rich, shutting down prisons, doxxing the police—vigilante acts of justice that saw the only acceptable equivalent to storming the Winter Palace today as bombing the data-warehousing systems at Google. If politics is downstream from culture, then here was a culture that wanted to topple regimes.

In his interview with Haiduk, Popović states, "We seek out what might be a motivating factor for people—above all, young people."

I would also wonder what motivates young people, because even as a young person myself, these motivations eluded me. Throughout the years, I don't really know what it was that compelled me to join a demonstration. Five years after the fee-hike protests, I remember exiting the building where I worked in New York, and opening the door onto a procession of thousands who came to mourn the death of Eric Garner. People held signs that read "I Can't Breathe" and "Don't Shoot" and "Black Lives Matter." That night, the largest funeral in the city's recent memory was happening on the streets, from the fountains of Washington Square, down Madison Square Park to the churches past Houston Street, past the outdoor fish markets in Chinatown and westward to the river. I cried that night, and at Zucotti Park, and when I scrolled through Twitter images of the TOMA vehicles at Occupy Gezi in the neighborhoods I used to live in. I cried when Trump was elected, but not during the Women's March. I was emotionally depleted by then, yet still had so much more to learn. I would parrot the call and response of, "Tell Me What Democracy Looks Like," compensating with emotion that I could not rationalize was more than, at best, a tangential subplot for direct political action, yet simultaneously, I would wonder: after the protests are over, what happens to *all this?* What happens to all the anger, the stunted desire, the gathering thunderclouds of our generation's discontents, our grievances and our nursed alienations? Where does all of that energy go? I never found the answer, but I can tell you at least one thing: it doesn't go nowhere.

7.

During this time, I sat on literary panels, gave speeches at weddings, made orange chicken for holiday potlucks, and responded to emails on time. I kept up with the culture, went to Venice for the Biennale, signed up for Apple Music the week Frank Ocean dropped *Boys Don't Cry*. At Café Loup, I had dinners with my agent and editor, where we gossiped about how the state of the culture wars was translating into the latest sales figures from a publishing industry still gridlocked between Ivy League Leftists and Pulitzer Prize Winners of Color. Culture, as we conceptualized it, was still some version of liberal pageantry, reinforced by the reigning mood of the Obama years, and parcelled out into marketing categories formulated on the syrupy promises of racial diversity and visibility politics. We didn't think it would end, until it became inconceivable to believe that we'd ever thought it could last.

When exactly did the Obama years end? Somewhere between Gamergate and the shooting of Michael Brown.

When I think about the Obama years, I think about a giant party that didn't want to end. But at some point, the party always ends, never on a high note, but at some blurry point in the morning, when the dance floor thins out, the lights fade on, and you look around to see that nobody's in the same mood as they were in before. Sometimes, all I could ever be certain about was the mood. During the lead-up to the election, all I knew was that the "aura" was changing. A darkening energy clouded over New York. I remember arriving at a furniture sale in Brooklyn hosted by two friends of mine who were decamping to Finland. We opened the windows and cleansed the place with palo santo, and talked about how the mood in the US was souring—it didn't "feel safe." People were getting restless. I remember getting my Tarot card reading done by a practicing Wiccan I knew, who told me that bad fortune would come if I stayed in New York, and I should leave for Berlin "sooner than later." Incredibly, I couldn't get my mind off the blood moon prophecies from the Book of Joel about four lunar eclipses that would fall in two consecutive years, triggering the Second Coming of Christ. In the past, I may have dismissed this as pure lunacy, but by the time the eleventh hour came, I no longer did.

When the time came for the unspeakable, people claimed it was inevitable. People pointed fingers. (The media! Identity politics!) Demons were getting excised. Then after the flagellation came the narratives. The Russia investigations. The Wylie hearings. Collectively, we appealed to the prophets to tell us what went wrong. What were the warning signs? How did this happen? And at some point or other, we privately asked ourselves: were we surprised?

8.

In 2014, Christopher Wylie was twenty-four, the year he came up with the idea to mine millions of Facebook profiles for private and personal information that could create psychographic political profiles in what he termed, in the *Guardian*, as Cambridge Analytica's "psychological warfare mindfuck tool."

I first read about Wylie in 2018, when I saw him in a photo shoot for the *Guardian*, with pink hair and a nose ring, wearing a camouflage jacket. It's possible his outfit is the whole reason why he caught my attention, so influential were those details on my thinking, my language, that I texted a hair stylist I knew if he could dye my hair "Wylie pink."

Wylie became, for me, an aspirational figure for the culture, a generational hero: the whistleblower. Before Cambridge Analytica, Wylie worked in Canadian Parliament for the opposition party, and as a data analyst for Obama's national director. After, Wylie was approached by Alexander Nix, the head of Cambridge Analytica, who told him "We'll give you total freedom. Experiment. Come and test out all your crazy ideas," which bred the kind of analytics that revealed, for instance: "people who liked 'I hate Israel' on Facebook also tended to like Nike shoes and KitKats."

I never ended up dying my hair, forgot I ever wanted to, but was then reminded when I discovered this detail, which stopped me in my tracks: at the time when Alexander Nix discovered him, Wylie was enrolled at the London School of Economics for a "PhD in fashion forecasting."

"Politics is like fashion," said Wylie in an early meeting with Steve Bannon. "Trump is like a pair of Uggs, or Crocs, basically," he said. "So how do you get from people thinking 'Ugh. Totally ugly' to the moment when everyone is wearing them?" After meeting Bannon, Wylie was soon introduced to Robert Mercer, Cambridge Analytica's billionaire investor, and his daughter Rebekah Mercer.

When he met them in Rebekah Mercer's Manhattan apartment, she stated, "Oh we need more of your type on our side!" by which she meant, "the gays," Wylie clarified.

Bannon also saw "the gays," said Wylie, as "early adopters," believing that once the gays were on board, "everyone else will follow," explaining why he was "so into the whole Milo thing."

This was the level of detail I imagined, once plumbed deep enough, might unlock for me the absurdity that could work as an organizing principle of the era. Absurdity was the only operational logic behind things like Yiannopoulos' "Gays For Trump" party at the Republican National Convention, for which he created promotional posters of shirtless twinks wearing Make America Great Again hats. When asked, in *Bloomberg Businessweek*, why he surrounds himself with white supremacists and 4Chan trolls, he explained, "Because they're interesting." Here influencers served as energy for energy's sake, the libidinal compass at the heart of the Breitbart Doctrine, which sees no qualitative difference between fascist leader and hip-hop celebrity. "Radical" denoted anything that hit a base common denominator of shocking or offensive, regardless of discernible political affiliation. Transgression for transgression's sake.

A deference to the "radical" as a blanket aesthetic, erasing any discernible political coordinates, would also be the logic behind then editor Tina Brown's deciding to put Donald Trump on the cover of *Vanity Fair* in 1994, as the kind of "authentic bullshit," she recounted after Trump was elected, which "epitomized the brassy craziness of the times."

By the 2016 election, brassy craziness had crossed irretrievably into the insane. Around this time, *Breitbart* began accompanying its articles about Yiannopoulos with an itemized list of his clothing worn in photo shoots, brands that include jackets from Balmain and suits from Gieves and Hawkes, outfitting Yiannopoulos as a socialite in his own right. Fashion was politics, politics was fashion. After a while, such absurdity was no longer the organizing principle but the animating force behind a culture industry led by a handful of influencers who were systemically incentivized to parrot back to the culture, as entertainment, the worst narratives it could tell about itself.

9.

Facebook, a monopolist marketing platform that socially-conditions a third of the world's population under an ethos of "connecting people" at neocolonial proportions, is the most powerful arm of what Dena Yago describes in *e-flux* as "the content industrial complex." The phrase refers to the system of corporate-sponsored media designed with compulsively clickable headlines and images that compel users to share it on social platforms, gluing users to their screens for long amounts of time that said social platforms can then sell back to corporations who are often also the ad sponsors for the media originally being circulated. In this system, users aren't the customers so much as the livestock being sold, too dependent on the gamified apparatus of renewable bite-size stimulation to break away. "As a term," Yago writes, "'user' resonates unambiguously with the language of addiction."

Yago is a member of K-HOLE, the artist collective and mock trend-forecasting agency that analyzes the way certain trends emerge from the content circulated online. In 2013, K-HOLE released a trend report titled "Youth Mode: A Report on Freedom," commissioned by the Serpentine Gallery in London. The report opens with, "It used to be possible to be special," declaring a post-MTV marketing strategy that effectively neuters what used to be "special"—the idiosyncratic, indie—by recycling and monetizing emergent local trends into a mass-market aesthetics, made equally accessible to mall rats in Kentucky or radical queers in Manila. This tactic is known in advertising as "coolhunting." In an era when any emergent style trend can be poached by corporations, and marketed out to mass culture, K-HOLE asks how it might be possible to avoid detection, avoid commodification, avoid getting coolhunted. The solution is invisibility. Here, K-HOLE proposes a ubiquitous "youth mode," a quasi-fashion style adapted from Hito Steyerl's "withdrawal representation," identified by a normie aesthetic that was so undetectable, so camouflaged as to be boring, so bland that it could never be taken for "special" or "cool." It was the "anti-cool," demonstrating a chameleonic ability to blend with the surroundings on the ground, thriving below the radar of trend forecasting agencies in an age of big data algorithms and universal surveillance.

Thus: Normcore. It was a fashion trend defined as "situational," "adaptable," and "post-aspirational." By sporting Nike trainers, cargo shorts, and Gap pullovers, Normcore finds its identity in the incognito, in its ability to relate to any number of groups on any side of the culture. The aesthetic was spoofed in an episode of *Model Files*, a web series produced by the fashion retailer VFILES, where fictional (and real life) casting director Preston Chaunsumlit is shown outfitting underground style icons in Old Navy with its blanket mass-market aesthetics. The joke had reached its apex by the time Fiona Duncan wrote, in *New York* magazine, about Normcore, a style that captured "self-aware, stylized blandness" with an accompanying slideshow of models wearing "Uniqlo khakis with New Balance sneakers or Crocs." Here, the simulacrum merges perfectly with the real. In streetwear photos around SoHo, Chaunsumlit is photographed wearing "white nurse clogs" i.e. Crocs, a sort of de-facto icon for Normcore, until four years later Demna Gvesalia, the creative director of Vetements and Balenciaga, designed platform Crocs with pointed rhinestones and send them down the Balenciaga runway in Paris.

This is how "totally ugly" led to "fashion," how "fashion" led to "politics." Track the movement, gather the early-adopters. Dupe the public. Talking about all those gay early-adopters, I ended up meeting Chaunsumlit in 2016 at a gay party in Berlin called Cocktail d'Amore, a few weeks before we acted alongside each other in a web series for Berlin Biennale in the same exhibition that featured K-HOLE. This is an example of a coincidental detail I don't know where else to put. Most of this is just nonsense. I'm still waiting for someone, anyone, to piece together the relevant details, make this up into a coherent narrative, tell me a story.

Here are the notes. Where is the story?

10.

We tell ourselves stories in order to live. I understand this to be the literary equivalent of the pareidolia effect, or apophenia, the psychological phenomenon where the brain assorts unrelated stimuli into a coherent image, the completion of basic gestalt principles where none exist, or hearing what sounds like words as urine hits the water. As neural networks are only as strong as the data sets they are provided, the brain hunts for what it already knows, or what makes sense to previous sets before assimilating to an encounter with the new. During these years I would struggle with understanding that not everything is meaningful, not every coincidence is interesting, or would eventually become "the story," with enough lead time for the hindsight bias to emerge.

Here's another irrelevant chain of associations: I first met Elizabeth Spiers in 2013 at an online publication called *Flavorwire*, where she was hired to revamp its digital strategy, which consisted of selling ad impressions, and partnering with advertisers to produce custom events and email giveaways. Two years earlier, Spiers was a writer for *Forbes* around the same time I was also at *Forbes* writing book reviews. For the October 2011 issue, Spiers profiled Arianna Huffington, who was featured on the cover as one of the world's "100 Most Powerful Women."

Here, Spiers had been the first to break, in detail, the revenue strategy on which Huffington built her digital empire at *The Huffington Post*, and by 2010 had grown to a total of 6,000 unpaid bloggers and 186 paid staffers. The model embodied a bottom-up content model distributed across twenty special-interest verticals ranging from US News and Business to Relationships and Wellness, built off a similar model as *Gawker*, which Spiers founded in 2005.

Two years after *Huffington Post* moved from analog to digital, Andrew Breitbart, who was co-founder and partner of the *Huffington Post* in 2005, "decided to go out and create our media," he said in 2004, and launched *Breitbart News*. Since its inception, it was funded by Robert and Rebekah Mercer who also funded Cambridge Analytica. *Breitbart* would become responsible for publishing and promoting political content in conjunction with, on the one hand, Cambridge Analytica, and on the other, conservative pollster Pat Caddell, who said he worked on the Trump campaign because he was looking for someone with the name recognition and the resources that could connect with voter bases disillusioned by the establishment. In a reference to *Mr. Smith Goes to Washington*, Caddell stated in the *New Yorker*, "He clearly wasn't the best Smith, but he was the *only* Smith."

Before *Flavorwire*, Elizabeth Spiers was fired as the editor in chief of the *New York Observer* by Jared Kushner, owner of Observer Media Group, and future senior advisor to his father-in-law, President Trump. In an official statement, Kushner lauded Spiers for launching "a slew of new verticals and web properties, and invigorat[ing] the newsroom." By the time Spiers had been hired to launch verticals and invigorate the newsroom at *Flavorwire*, I had been working as a books reporter, and edited an author interview series for which I asked questions like "What was the last good book you read?" and "Where do you think American fiction is headed," before I was fired by Spiers after just three interviews, because I failed to make any newsbreak anyone cared about.

Forbes, *The Huffington Post*, *Gawker*, *Breitbart*, *Flavorwire*, and *The New York Observer* were all publications that belonged to the same generation of digital media in the 2000s that specialized in sub-800 word viral content that abounded in listicles, affective slideshows, Op-Eds, and identitarian politics, that was designed for the explicit purpose of being shared widely on social media. The content that I wrote for *Flavorwire* didn't drive up page views, but instead was understood as "legacy content" that lost money, but would boost the overall reputation of the site, which I failed to do.

Clearly, I was missing something fundamental. Here, the publication is treated like an organism, whose political platform was only as strong as its ability to communicate to the culture its survival of the most frequently shared on social—an essentially ad-backed profit model sustained by corporations as part of a revenue system that itself spawned but also precipitated the collapse of an American news culture already in decline. How the inauguration of the content industrial complex paved the way for Trump to troll his way to the White House, one social share at a time, might be an example of a "bigger picture" story, but I'm too late here, having failed to grasp even the general idea at the time, probably *the* times, the generation, whatever. Where any of these people are today, I have no idea. I assume they moved on after the damage was done. After a certain point, the only thing to do, which was also the most difficult, was to move on as well.

11.

Somehow, I cannot. After the shouting in the hall, the revenue reports, my neurosis, my paranoia, and my racial biases, I haven't found the through-line to make this story work. What's left are a series of fragmentary images that, if viewed in quick succession, might appear as a comprehensible stop-motion for the times. The reality is harder to grasp. These days I see panic at the borders, riots in Paris, Twitter bot armies posing as civilians and civilians posing as prophets armed with AR-15 semiautomatic rifles, and I still don't know what it is I'm looking at. These days, I'm often advised to just relax. After I was discharged from the psychiatric hospital, I was diagnosed with "unspecified psychosis," and told that I'd shown symptoms of PTSD and schizophrenia: conspiracy theories, paranoia, hallucinations, delusions of grandeur—symptoms that did not otherwise strike me as unreasonable for these years, when insanity is the only sane response to an insane world. How I got here, I have no idea. Here's what I do know: that I still have difficulties trusting people, don't like crowds, keep searching inside my brain for my one proverbial "voice" while I find nothing but an index of the chaos already known.

Some day, I will have to learn when to stop asking questions. That not every signal was meant for me, and I have to be okay with not knowing the endings of things. In the months after discharge, I spent a lot of time swimming in my parents' pool in California, staring into the space between two palm trees where there used to be a third, which had to be cut down because of termites. At my father's suggestion, I sometimes tied a swimming belt around my waist, attached to a column beneath the balcony, and practiced swimming in place. Flailing my limbs in water while making no progress at all is where I'm at these days. Because everywhere my mind turns, I keep looking for the newsbreak, but I just keep moving in circles. I flush out my bad juju with higher-frequency energy and thoughts that serve me. I sit in the sunshine, meditate. On the phone, I listen as my friend tells me about how time is a linear concept for "occupying the material plane," and by negotiating with past lives, I might find a path to "ascension." This I recognize, in so many words, as an appeal to the spiritual, which I am looking for. Because after I stopped believing in God, I stopped believing in the story. No more meaning, no narrative. All that comes back to me now are my heaps of broken images.

I used to believe that as a writer, I had to open myself up, like a compact mirror, to the generation, but when my generation became intolerable, so did I. Now where did that get me? I still wonder about the people I used to know, whatever came of the conversation at *The Standard*, whether any of the protesters I knew ended up in jail, or about the office assistant I knew at *Flavorwire* who one day, in New York, sold all her possessions and moved to Texas to sell 3D-printed rifles through Defense Distributed. She eventually became the organization's director, and CEO of a company called Ghost Gunner. In a press release about her new role, she is also described as "organizing several independent spoken word nights and artist showcases."

Mostly I try not to think about these things. Most of the people I know carried on less controversial lives. They published novels, exhibited at Basel, got married, started their own record label, or quit their jobs at declining publications and rebranded themselves by learning how to code. If I followed suit, I would also move on and live a functional life, and eventually I will. I'll let go of my questions upon questions, releasing them into this deluge of aborted narratives. Because there is nowhere left to put them. Where else are they supposed to go? Where do they all end up? I haven't found the answer yet, but I can give you a hint: they don't go nowhere.

Five Poems

Collateral Damage & **The First People**—*for Marlene Dumas*
& **Coping Strategies** & **Words to Say it**
& **And God Became a Monkey**—*for Hannah Höch*

Astrid Alben

Collateral Damage

Poet hadn't yet made Earth the jobless vigorously typed
not yet news bulletins absolutes weren't yet accident prone

lunatics all wore the same garments no one cockgobbled
a shame not yet sodomites thought love declarations were

daylight saving lies coughed politely from the wings. Words
standing still before Poet stood still a harelipped giant bowing

his head before the mountain in so doing paid homage
to the mountain patiently rivers down its sides.

The First People
for Marlene Dumas

Your credibility is shot through the opposite
beautiful smearkisses on every bit of I'm asleep

to the question *are you asleep* or no awake to the same
lullaby then asks incredulously *really awake?*

Rudderless coochy coo tumbles through a bottomless
process like colony collapse everything rotting

dehydrating & disintegrating decomposes the universe
no end a colossal baby trying to climb out of its cunt.

Coping Strategies

Poet takes some après-ski delight in the departure lounge
beyond his reflection tarmac his suitcase on a baggage trailer

I see he packed shoelaces camouflage. Backup. Indistinctly one
origami swan gathers up its quills accelerates on the runway

halfway announces shutters down for take off behind a decorative fern a
television honks its head off information a non-local

quantity. Ink *everywhere*. Skidding would be catastrophic Poet observes
cautiously lost cohesion. Better flight before light.

Words to Say it

Washed-up language perplexed itself a squawking birdie from the
nest fall brainwaves crack & compromises Poet

alone stand. Haemorrhaging nouns the modal to its end send.
Whoa! Steady please! Lieber! Lieder! Lei—der

my mouth wend wi—der Dichter plunges capacity expansion
with his epileptic tonsil tickler pushes down

gender splendour soapsuds coursing through Poet's migrant heart
his utter udder other my spacetime ladder.

And Became a Monkey
for Hannah Höch

On tiptoe I follow God around his classroom as he
resumes his rebuttal of Poet's attributes—leniency

the persistent rumours he's cockalorum & the one where we're
nihilistic thoughts that come into his tra-la-la

hand in his pocket jangles a spectrum of promises most
memorable of which monkey-twitch is Poet's inside our

heads like a pinball machine with flippers going balls knocking
the bumpers playing I don't know *et voilà*.

Nebraska

Nathan Dragon

He loved her even though she was always doing something, Not *allll* the way right, as he put it and he never giving her the time. Time enough before he could say, Know what I mean.

Not all the way right like nothing wrong but nothing that makes it easier.

And she loved him back even though he wasn't ever right himself and tended towards difficulty.

Things were what's the matter.

They thought about these things, each to their own respective selves, quiet in a truck stop motel in Nevada. How they loved each other so much and the sound of the other breathing, their breathing, in a room they'll probably never be back to.

No, wait, it wasn't Nevada. He had never been to Nevada, he'll say later on when recalling this. It was Nebraska. They were in between.

And she'd say, Nope—nah uh, they'd never been to Nebraska.

They held each other tightly on their way, stopped off in the middle for now. Somebody out there knows the place.

Getting there.

He could picture her in the different lights of where they had been before and she was imagining the things he used to do, and that he'd do them again, if he could just remember himself well enough so he could be sure.

Three Pages
Sarah Boulton

I spent several months glancing with my head and eyes to my left while driving past a strange pink hotel courtyard that had *three peacocks* in it. Sometimes they were there, sometimes they were not. I started to do it religiously. The glance became more sophisticated. Sharp. The blue and the green of the peacocks was always a blur. Wind down your window, I said only a few times. It was private. A collection of the speed of the colours of blue and green. I've thought about for what seemed like forever. Thought and thought about it.

You can't force delicacy

Can you identify the dove in the wild?

No

Why not?

I would not like to commission a candle that is the same size as my neck but find one that is.

*

I have learned that you are able to give yourself goosebumps in any situation, just by thinking about it. I have an artwork that is in progress. I am thinking a lot lately about the experience of looking at rows of trees with even gaps between them. Like breaths between, faraway. Someone walks between the trees, breathing out into each gap, while I drive in the distance with a single audience member sitting next to me in the car. We drive in a loop usually. I tell them that someone is walking and breathing in this way during the drive, although I am not sure exactly where. There are many types of these rows of trees. My idea is that you would hand out paper flyers to people, inviting them to be the passenger, with goosebumps on your arms.

Five Columns

Sascha Macht, *translated by* Amanda DeMarco

From late 2018 to early 2019, Sascha Macht was the writer-in-residence at a castle in the German city of Beeskow. As part of his appointment, Macht was required to write a weekly column for the *Märkische Oderzeitung*, a regional newspaper in eastern Brandenburg. The *Märkische Oderzeitung*, in turn, was required to print whatever he sent them.

Renate Kanter

I finally visited Renate Kanter in a nursing home at the edge of Bad Saarow, where she has lived for some years. Her room is small, and her treasures are stacked on two sets of shelves in the corner: colorfully printed boxes, each of them filled with maps, dice, meeple, instructions, and tiny tokens. Renate Kanter is the grande dame of complex conflict simulation, in which historical or fictional military operations can be experienced in the form of a board game on your living room table. For more than forty years she's done nothing but develop these games, some of which have become classics with a limited but enthusiastic following, e.g. "Storming St. Egidien," "Courland Isn't Answering," "The Tank with the Blue Eyes," and "Red Moon over Samarkand."

There's coffee, pretzel sticks, and poppyseed cake as I sit with her on the sofa. Renate Kanter doesn't speak, at least not to other people. Her language has always been that of war and games, a challenging combination, which confronts us in every part of her simulations, in the relationship between intelligence and morality, strategy and decision, coincidence and luck, victory and defeat.

On the coffee table, she's spread out the prototypes for her new, yet unnamed work, perhaps her last. She must have worked on the concept for months and calculated thousands of possible moves. She painted and glued together her cardboard and wooden materials with the help of her nurse Jonas. I observe: a gigantic map with a dark center, perhaps depicting Eastern Europe and part of Central Asia. The instructions, written up on a typewriter, reveal: Every player takes on the role of a tiny national entity, which has recently declared its independence from a powerful central government. Now the goal is to strengthen your own economy, fight corruption, form alliances, and rebuff the attacks of the former motherland together. However, it is conceivable that one player could secretly make a pact with the central government, in order to gain military and economic advantages for themselves over their competitors. A sinister, quiet game, consisting of street fighting, industrialization, organized crime, and the intrigues of secret services. Renate Kanter shrugs when I ask her when it will be finished.

On the drive back to Beeskow, I think over what title I would give to this work. "Rise and Fall of the Soviet Empire"? "Steppe and Shadows"? "Wolves Eat the Dogs"? "Death and Rebirth"? Through games, we understand the world. Dark and rain-swept is the country I am driving through.

Some Things that Don't Exist

A FILM THAT WAS NEVER MADE

The World as Will and Imagination. A man thinks that he is a door and falls in love with a woman who thinks she's a window. The two moves into a house together, where they realize that their new abode is actually a group of people, friends who believe that they are a house. A great hubbub. At the end, Kevin Costner appears in the form of a revivalist preacher who claims to be a river and explains that all of the proceedings depicted in the film are based on a true story.

A BOARD GAME NEVER PLAYED

Kicking Up a Fuss in Heinzmannsdorf. When, in the titular locality, the lights go out, the players, in the form of a band of imps, begin to make all sorts of rude mischief in the lanes. No one wins or loses at the end of the match, because when the time comes, all of them have long been sitting in complete confusion around the board, which is buried under hundreds of figures, disks, marbles, dice, coins, and cards. What a surly lot of fun!

A BOOK THAT WAS NEVER WRITTEN

A Novel Without People. Nothing but extensive descriptions of natural events, animals, uninhabited architecture, ownerless things. A masterpiece of poetic contemplation and a coup against the psychologizing outgrowths of a literature that constantly pushes the individual and their little problems to the centre of the narrative. Only a bit tiring now and again.

AN OBJECT NEVER USED

Are you in the possession of a wooden töftel? If so: good for you! I've heard that if you lay this small, round thing over the bridge of your nose, all sadness vanishes. Sadly, I haven't been able to try it out myself—wooden töftel are hard to come by nowadays.

A COMIC NEVER DRAWN

The Danish Lantern is about the courier Aksel Hansen, who, after a collision with an enchanted traffic light, develops the ability to turn into a living-room floor-lamp. Together with his best friend, the talking raccoon dog Thomas, he gets wise to the scheme of the avaricious orthodontist Dr. Nørregård, who wants to put overpriced braces on all of the children of Copenhagen.

A GOD NO ONE BELIEVES IN

Let's call him Bob. He's the patron saint of gravel, mayflies, and party hats—an inconspicuous, friendly fellow who spends his free time looking through the trash for bottles with refundable deposits. It's said that in a few forgotten corners of the world there are a few befuddled old birds, drinkers, handbag snatchers, and daydreamers who direct their prayers to him before they go to sleep, but that's nothing more than a rumour.

Märkische Heide[1]

Steam rises between the lemon trees. The ponds and canals are clear but toxic. The salamanders, water sprites, and snails in them speak an incomprehensible dialect. At night, the glowing coaches of international caravans rumble past. Those who enter on foot via the road from the north east must pay a toll: a haunch of venison. Many villages here were built on posts in the bog. The larger cities are woven with dense network of steam pipes, ropeways, and pulley systems. In summer drunken wastrels stroll through the sparse birch groves.

A writing wayfarer once spoke of how this country is like the board of a game played with dice made from frozen blood.

The remote farms, mobile home courts, Rundlings, and garden cities bear names such as "Strg Alt Del Golm," "Terrortal," "Stalinhüttenstadt," "Neu Tokio," "Bad Golfplatz," "Superzelle," "Preußisch Blau," or "Drehdichweg."[2] A former biogas plant is a karaoke bar today, gold panners doze on a bench in front of the German Unity Bar and Hotel, a pack of childlike ghosts have just taken up residence in an abandoned roadside service area, and music festivals, weddings, and court proceedings take place on the military parade grounds. If you come from the southwest on the magnetic monorail, you'll ride once around a forested shield volcano with a smouldering crater known as "Old Boss." At the beginning of spring, the Soviet combat tanks thaw in the asparagus fields. Calendars haven't caught on here, and so the dreadful question poses itself: what time do we find ourselves in? A cautious answer: perhaps just before the end of the world, perhaps 2019 BC, perhaps at the end of the midday nap.

Manor houses are found throughout the country, erected by an extra-terrestrial civilization from the farthest edge of the Milky Way. On the shore of the flooded gravel pit, a motorcycle gang suns itself in the grass. Around the afternoon coffee hour, a trio disguised as sunflowers holds up the branch savings bank on the market square. If you take a close look, from the highest garbage heap at the scrapyard, you can make out two moons in the night sky: the one as if soaked in schnapps, the other the eye of the divine chinchilla. The lie was born in this country just as the truth was, poverty as well as wealth, wholehearted nonsense as well as dangerous monkey business, sorrow as well as mirth. Large dogs are sometimes treated with more dignity here than certain old persons.

Flat, vast, barren, narrow, blossoming landscapes.[3] Day-care centers. Saw works. Zoos for local fauna. Crashed spaceships. Supermarkets. A few truly beautiful gardens inhabited by werewolves.

---

1 Märkische Heide is a municipality in Germany; it is also the song of the state of Brandenburg; see https://www.youtube.com/watch?v=h9fytYjC6FQ.

2 "Strg Alt Del Golm"; *Terror Valley*; "Stalinhüttenstadt"; *New Tokyo*; *Bad Golfcourse*; *Supercell*; *Prussian Blue*, or *Getoutofhere*.

3 "Blühende Landschaften," or *blossoming landscapes*—Helmut Kohl's 1990 prediction for the economies of the newly reunited eastern states.

Von der Stille

I'm being followed. Recently while walking through the city, I thought I saw a figure from the corner of my eye, in the narrow lane between St. Mary's Church and Breite Straße.

I call him Dietrich von der Stille, sometimes also "The Cyclops." What he calls himself and what others call him, I don't know. Where he comes from, why he does whatever—a mystery.

But I know that he subsists on sniffing mumia, a substance made from the ground remains of ancient Egyptian mummies, Chinese corpses mummified in honey, or northern European bog bodies, used as a remedy into the twentieth century. I also know that in the winter of 1944, he was in attendance at the castle of the vampiric vom Stein family in southern Hungary, together with a few nefarious German doctors, in order to decipher the secret of immortality. Additionally to be found in my notes is the information that Axl Rose, front-man of the hard-rock band Guns N' Roses, once expressed the grotesque wish to be the commander of an army in the depths of the rainforests of Guatemala—I'm certain that Dietrich von der Stille really was such a commander, who hunted members of the indigenous Ixil population during the Guatemalan Civil War.

It's not just writers, underworld bosses, and chimney sweeps, but every person is surrounded by dark, indeterminate things, signs, and occurrences: fear, conflict, misfortune, sadness. Poetry's significant advantage lies in its revealing of the unknown in plain view. It allows us to have dealings with it.

Once I wrote of a flying carpet that brought me to the peak of a mountain, where I hoped to discover the visage of evil, but there was nothing at all on the mountain, and so I looked down, dumbstruck, at the wide world lying below me.

Once I dreamed I was lost in an endless vault under the earth. Through narrow windows, light fell into the passageways and chambers, but I couldn't manage to reach their filth-smeared panes. I was carrying a burning candle, my only comfort. I walked farther and farther, steadfast in the thought of eventually getting out. Only when the flame went out did I once again find myself on the shore of a black lake under a grey sky.

Once Dietrich von der Stille called me on my phone He said that our entire universe was located in a single drop of sweat falling from the bodies of two wrestling and simultaneously copulating Titans. As I hung up, my heart was full of tender fright.

Dreams and Relations

In 1857, the poet Charles Baudelaire described the world as "an oasis of horror in a desert of boredom." The writer Roberto Bolaño took this sentence as a motto to preface his novel collection *2666*, that massive, winding panorama of literature, madness, love, and the unfathomable criminality resulting from the drug war on the Mexican-American border. What do Baudelaire's words mean? That reality is no joke—nor is literature.

In the literary universe of the horror writer H.P. Lovecraft, unknown evil gods from the icy depths of the cosmos determine the destiny of time and space. The ninety-nine rooms in the Paris apartment building on rue Simon-Crubellier, whose contents the writer and Holocaust survivor Georges Perec describes in detail in his novel *Life: A User's Manual*, are filled with the fates of their still-living or long-dead inhabitants. In Bolaño's text "A Stroll Through Literature," he says: "I dreamt that Earth was finished. And the only human being to contemplate the end was Franz Kafka. In heaven, the Titans were fighting to the death. From a wrought-iron seat in Central Park, Kafka was watching the world burn." When Lovecraft died in 1937, Perec had just turned two. The science-fiction writer Philip K. Dick died on March 2 1982, Perec a day later after a long stay in Brisbane, the actor John Belushi two days later. On March 3 1982, the day of Perec's death, the future actress Jessica Biel was born in Ely, Minnesota. Franz Kafka is still alive today, a tiny 135-year-old man, hidden in the back room of a shop for sports apparel in Alice Springs, in the middle of dried-out nowhere, Australia. 2666 minus 1982 is 684: the meagre remains of the never-completed submarine U-684, commissioned by the German navy in 1941, were sunk in the harbour of Hamburg a few days before the capitulation of the Third Reich.

Literature dreams. It dreams of life and of death, of life without death, and of the endlessness of death. It dreams of the beginning, the progression, and the end of time. In the dream of literature only two people attain immortality: its author and its reader, both lost in the desert on a cold, lonely planet between the stars.

Roberto Bolaño, who has been dead since 2003, writes: "I dreamt that Georges Perec was three years old and visiting my house. I was hugging him, kissing him, saying what a sweet boy he was."

Four Poems

Making Sausages & **Mermaid Outing** & **Butterfield** & **Marissa**

Hannah Regel

Making Sausages

The family room is full of dead deer. The family are proud of what they have killed but the girls who've come to stay are not proud for them they think it's gross, their faces tell us so. They talk about how they do not like the dead deer or the family that has killed the deer as they break the family swimming pool apart with sledgehammers. They are wearing inappropriate footwear as they break the pool. The oldest boy in the family laughs at them he thinks they are dumb and he tells them so he spoils their hair extensions when they aren't looking. They shout Hey Mister I don't care how many protein shakes egg whites you've eaten I'll Kill You I've done it before I'll do it again you better believe it. The girls need money. Family friend Randy has a sausage shop. They decide the girls will spend a day working for Randy and that is how they will pay for petrol. Their outfits are all wrong for making sausage but it charms. They ask for pink aprons and get blood on their shoes and ankles. They slice the belly and the liver whilst talking about foie gras. The girls like that, they say. For the money shot they spray minced meat on the walls and the floor. There is meat everywhere it is on their cheeks and on the clock. They get a can of dog food out from the back of the car and fill a pig's intestine with it. It is for the oldest boy, it will show him. They sell the sausages they have made by the side of the road. They hand the sausages through car windows with their bare hands and show their breasts to the drivers as they lean. They save the dog food sausage, though, don't sell that. Setting it aside in a plastic bag they say This One's Special. They take it home and feed it to the oldest boy. He doesn't know it is dog food and he likes it, he smiles. The girls look directly into the camera, they say Don't Mess With Us. They drive a pink truck to the next town

Mermaid Outing

The girls are paid to babysit for a woman they have just met in a car park. They tell the girl they are babysitting to say Ass she says No they say Do It. The little girl says Ass and then she says Bitch. The girls give the girl they are sitting a makeover. They smear makeup all over her face it looks bad they are sort of laughing at her while they do it. After this they are bored. They decide to play hide and seek. The little girl's mother comes back and asks where her daughter is. The girls say they don't know. It is very dark when this happens and they are in the woods.

Butterfield

No one being able to recognise a door
we crack our noses and discard the shell
the night blows a dust into our skulls
writing our middle-years backwards
   Wake up to the engine of shoulders, perfect lips
   and my stomach kissing your back all big and full of wine
Can you do 7 days, 2 doubles? I mean I'd rather do nothing ever
just exist as scattered images already applauded, But Sure
when can I start? I'll need the money for raising horses
and building catapults for more permanent acts
define permanence, define catapult
pay all my bills, compost, what else
being gorgeously useless and full of it
   she said: I Am The Most Important Artist of My Generation
   then later, amended: Female Artist
She was wearing a big fashionable white shirt with a window for her bra in the back
spilt wine all over it and was talking loudly and I wanted to be her
I want to be the person that spills wine all over their shirt
and still says things to the party like: I Am The Most Important Artist
to do what I want which is real
Elizabeth Taylor's posture
now that is a big Fuck You question mark
her curling shoulders, they just mean it
like Whiskey. Steal a mink
write No Sale on the big mirror
I wish
Sure, it was me that stuck the finger in but How Dare He:
with the grit fist of his rightness make a hole in our boat
the calloused hand of honesty
cringes in the raft
getting salt in the pact.
She goes back to him, Liz
and besides I love him
I wash my feet in the leaks eating sorry toffee
I would never punch a hole in a wall because there is no evil inside me
A lie. There is plenty.
Example: I would never punch a hole in a wall
I am too vain to move my body in ways that make it animal
this is a kind of evil because I am an animal. I am. See:
just yesterday I dropped a fish finger on the floor
because no one was there to see it fall I put it on his plate not mine: my animality
it sits in its avoidance, in making other people dirty
there is a kind of pleasure

Marissa

Obedience
reserves light
into the skin
or shaved spots
of cradling pain
plucked eyebrows
visible hips
and hi hi hi
her mother
a martyr
sits alone
on a garden chair
everyone's
an actress
at 2pm
where
the days
are silent
because
they are
full

Twenty-Three and Me

Andrew Lampert

Last year we bought my father a DNA kit for his birthday. These are the relatives we've found so far:

1. A gorgeous Lower East Side pickle vendor's daughter who dropped out of the third grade because she needed prescription glasses that her family could not afford. She never learned to read and died of diphtheria, which she contracted from her first kiss. Her despondent parents had no money for a graveyard burial so they sold her corpse to a medical school.

2. A barbershop quartet singing bigamist haberdasher with two wives, two separate families, and two dogs, one at each house, both named Bandit.

3. A stereotypically rich hook-nosed Jewish banker who lived in a large house filled with goblets and bags of gold. He prized his many Torahs, rare books and antiquarian manuscripts above all, however he perpetually lamented the difficulties of fitting oversized publications onto shelves. Remembered for his generosity and despair.

4. A hand towel salesman with no fixed address who collapsed in a Romanian sauna from complications related to a severely ingrown toenail. His pants and wallet were stolen from the changing room, and as a result no one ever knew his name or claimed his body, which was tossed into an open grave on the outskirts of the village where a pack of ravenous coyotes ate him to the bone.

5. A department store clerk who once sold a pair of diamond earrings to Mae West while she was in town with her touring play *Diamond Lil*. In her early twenties she briefly dated Ike Sewell, the inventor of Chicago deep dish pizza, who she recalled as being "cheap" and "handsy." Two days after the tragic death of her parents in a train accident, she married a door-to-door vacuum salesman who was strung out on speed-laced diet pills.

6. A Lithuanian coffin maker with low self-esteem who had difficulties collecting money from the grieving families who purchased his boxes. He slept in a hay-lined coffin under a horse hide blanket made from his childhood steed. Resentful villagers considered him to be extravagantly rich and spread unsavory, unverified rumors about his carnal relations with the dead.

7. A bald monocle-wearing architect in Jeleniewo, Poland who specialized in castle additions. Very pretentious. Married and divorced his first cousin, twice. Built a faulty bridge that collapsed and killed twenty-two people, including his own color-blind son.

8. A redheaded, green-eyed bricklayer who came back to work drunk after lunch and accidentally killed a coworker. Conditions on the site were deemed unsafe and he was ultimately acquitted for the murder, but the guilt of it all sent him into a spiral. Spiritually and mentally adrift, he quit his job and took off on a soul-searching journey to India. After wandering for three years he moved back to the US and settled in Indianapolis where he opened the city's first Indian food truck. At first things were slow but a glowing review on a midday news program and a two-for-one coupon in the Sunday paper prompted a business boom. Nearly a dozen customers were waiting in line when the truck's tandoori oven blew up, instantly killing him and also setting the Jamaican food truck parked in the adjoining spot ablaze, taking the life of the rheumatic eighty-three-year-old mother of the owner who came in that day to cover cash register duties for her granddaughter, who was still asleep in the basement apartment of the man who had impregnated her the night before.

9. A mother who had seven children and seven miscarriages with a philandering husband who never came back home from a trip to Siberia. Only three of the children survived past age seven, two were killed in two different wars at ages thirteen and fifteen. She died of exposure after a roving gang of thugs stole her only blanket one cold February night in Kiev.

10. A homewares store owner in the Bronx who sold bed sets, living room furniture, kitchen appliances, radios, televisions and stereo systems. In 1971 he personally sold a turntable to Clive Campbell, aka DJ Kool Herc, the first DJ and founding father of hip hop music. After leaving the store Campbell realized that he had been short changed by three dollars and fifty three cents.

11. A disgraced British butcher in Newcastle upon Tyne who was busted in a sting operation for selling llama meat, which he had been passing off to customers as organic free-range beef. When irritated customers complained that the meat didn't taste like beef he would try to convince them they were finally experiencing the real taste of beef, and that the

beef they were used to eating was artificial crap. The llamas were supplied by another cousin who also went to jail in a separate case after being found guilty of having sexual relations with llamas.

12. A restless Russian sheepherder with two different-colored eyes who refused to sleep indoors. He drank his own hot urine from a handmade thermos fashioned out of a goat's stomach. Never married.

13. A toupeed retiree who for the last eight years has spent a minimum of six hours each day at Guitar Center in Overland Park, Kansas playing only the higher end Fender Custom Shop guitars that the resentful clerks must specially unlock for him. Plugging into every amp on the floor, he constantly fiddles with the dials and in-board effects, picks out repetitious scales and patterns at varying speeds and volumes, never completes a whole song. Listening to customers testing out guitars, he will subtly start playing along, adding a solo or diminished seventh chords, hoping that they will notice and play in unison, or compliment him on his chops. He has never purchased anything at the store but once tried to return a gnarled cable without a receipt.

14. A chain-smoking human guinea pig whose skin became stained, soiled and burned after working for twenty-six years in a midtown Manhattan perfume factory that lacked proper ventilation. She is married to a former Tony Danza impersonator who currently works at Au Bon Pain at LaGuardia Airport.

15. A grossly overweight bully who became the third uniformed police officer in France, sworn into duty on March 13th, 1829. Later that night at Les Halles he also committed the first official act of police brutality. His wife was an eye-patch wearing barmaid who put up with constant fondling from customers. She lost her left eye in a failed attempt to break up a brawl and always smelled like grilled meat.

16. A lactose intolerant thirty-seven-year-old third grade schoolteacher from Cleveland who relocated to Haifa where she now teaches first grade. She has undiagnosed Tourette syndrome and is easily frustrated. If any of her students laugh or even smirk during her outbursts of obscenities they are instantly sent to the principal. She doesn't have a credit card.

17. A seventeenth century German alchemist who claimed in a gilded, self-printed book to have successfully turned lead into gold. In over 200 pages of dense, impenetrable writing he never explained his method, nor did he ever actually show his gold to anyone. He was widely mocked and ostracized by the other alchemists in his community, one of whom commented that the only magick he had performed was turning himself into a horse's ass.

18. An Estonian gravedigger, garlic farmer and notary. He was well known for being a whistling insomniac whose warbled lullabies wafted great distances in the dark night sky. Local legend had it that he once stayed awake for seven straight months. Short tempered and highly paranoiac, he refused to pay full price for any goods or services.

19. An anesthesiologist currently living in Tampa who explains everything to his patients with extended golf metaphors. Loves the water, can't swim.

20. A pair of bickering sisters, the older one blind, the younger one deaf. The blind sister was widowed after a horse stampede took her husband's life on the same evening as their marriage. The deaf sister, whose hair hung well past her knees, milled around the town well trading sexual favors for sips because she could not afford her own cup. The town children in the village came up with a naughty nursery rhyme about them that was sung for more than one hundred years after their death.

21. A Georgian poet and pimp who had four children with four whores, all of whom died before the age of two. His verse exclusively celebrated the autumnal equinox and khachapuri, the traditional cheese bread of Georgia. While none of his writings survive, an archive in the town of Akhalkalaki holds a rare and battered literary journal containing a particularly harsh review of his work, which is described as being *t'rak'uli* ("shitty") and the product of a *q'listava* ("dickhead").

22. A young woman whose village was burned by invaders, she narrowly escaped by running into the forest with her colicky thirteen-month-old daughter in a sling on her back. Her husband, who she had not seen for eleven months, was off somewhere fighting in the war, unaware that he was a first-time father. In the fury and confusion of the night she set the sleeping baby down for a second to catch her breath. Overcome by total exhaustion, she closed her eyes and fell instantly, deeply asleep.

Waking hours later with the morning light, she immediately discovered that the baby was missing. Had she crawled away deep into the forest? Panic-stricken, she spent five sleepless days searching in total agony before being discovered herself by a local farmer who, guesstimating that she was Jewish, stabbed her to death with a pickaxe.

23. A highly observant Orthodox jeweler in Argentina who lives with his covetous secular son and contemptuous daughter-in-law. He has survived multiple poisoning attempts without ever once considering that someone is trying to kill him. These near-death episodes are challenges of his faith, tests from God, or so he believes. Another assassination attempt is planned for New Year's Eve.

Notes on Happiness

Emmanuel Iduma

A school on the Island, the online newspaper reported, where a few devoted men, not more than seven each term, studied the God of water. How he turns water into wine, divides its onrush to reveal land; how he is dipped in it to fulfill or reveal righteousness; he it flows when he is pierced on the side; how it can't take the weight of a man, yet Peter walked afloat. Most of all, devotion: Daily exercise of looking at the sea, writing notes compelled by it, or placing feet in it. One with it: obsessed with immensity. How God is in expanse. He is curious about the men. He goes to the Island certain of nothing but to seek the sight of those who place their bodies in water, as worship.

Last night he returned to the city. This morning he walks to the church at the other end of his street. His back aches, a tiny knot that stays put even if he bends his back and presses a knuckle against it while guessing the spot. He considers the length of the street and how tired he is. What outweighs what? God or fatigue, body or spirit.

Then he sleeps a little. Can't remember, but once awake, alert and with reprieve, he knows he had spoken with his mother sometime earlier. He calls to confirm. You don't remember? No, I don't, he says. "You told me you would come this evening. Mind yourself and come here, or else." She laughs. He closes his eyes when he hears her laugh. The thrill he feels is as sharp and instant, as giving and ephemeral, as whatever happiness has come over her.

He drives, and there is unexpected traffic on the street abutting Ikorodu Road. As he waits to turn the bend, he hears a man whistle a tune, and he can swear it is Amadou. Am I sure of this, he wonders, not bothering to turn his face to the origin of the sound. Am I sure? Amadou had never whistled in memory. How does he attribute this sound to him—as though to trace in a crowd whose breath smells pleasant or foul, precise and peculiar, no margin of error.

Had he been to church, his mother asks. Yes. "It's good that you went even though you are tired." He takes the plate from her hand and sits. She tells him of her dream from the night before. Once she is finished, she asks him of the Island. "Did you enjoy yourself?" He shakes his head, a kind of ambivalence, and checks for the knot in his lower back. Come here, his mother says, ready to hold him, so he stands. In all this time he hasn't touched the food.

He sees in her eyes all the traces of her magnanimity toward him, lines of daily worry, how he may be moored. She is his mother, and this cannot simply be broached as the fact that she is a woman. In her tired eyes it is possible to imagine a distinction as such, woman and mother. Not always, not necessarily. But right now.

Driving back, another go-slow. He looks at the car beside his, a couple and their little girl. She has an iPad, playing a game, dodging underwater monsters, cruising her little fish. He sees this and feels as happy as he can manage today. But just as he smiles her mother grabs the iPad, mouths a warning. His face relaxes, surly.

An image of large water forms in his mind at once, and ah, yes, from his mother's dream. It is an aftereffect, a rendering of slow, broken time.

The Islanders haul Amadou's body from the sea. Those who look at the face, braised until bruised, rinsed in timeless salt, are hard-pressed to tell with their intent scrutiny in what belly he has undergone this passage. No one calls his name. They make an arc as they stand, gasping or grunting or howling. Once the arc is formed it stays sacrosanct, just as a grave for one is never marked for many. Those who eventually speak his name aloud have returned from the borderline of sea and land, where they saw his body. They sit two or more, or one, especially one, in distress over the long night, mesmerized by finality, and stunned by how, all along, they have been impervious to the faint dash separating is and was.

It's 3:45am when he wakes, and he is unable to fall back asleep. At least an hour passes. It's dread, not dream, a hovering. It's his life and Amadou's distinguished as memory, yet memory not past, as it leaps into what he has no other word for but now. Daily broken time. There is no innocence in dreams. Even benign ones—those in which he writes an email, speaks on the phone, throws a shirt in the laundry basket, grabs a mug—occur with sly purpose. These are not tentative moments, but final. In a dream he is spectator and protagonist. He is, at once, freed from responsibility for any action, and implicated in its consequence.

This morning you called my name. A male voice, yes—brother, friend, or father—but whose? A voice of my many childhoods and adulthoods, neither of which has run its course. It seems to me not a question of having heard you call me, but of all the voices that have spoken my name and have placed emphasis on the first two syllables. At the moment I hear you I am overtaken by sleep, by my benumbed body. Now I rise. Have you returned? What I miss most is what you might miss, me loving you. And so, whoever you are, bring me into this certainty: when I hear you I cannot mistake you for another.

His sister is on the phone. "I heard you came to the house." Oh, yes. "You couldn't wait to see me. See your big head." There is a pause, like a clearing, right where his laugh could have landed. "Are you okay?" He utters a remedial chortle, and her voice is back to normal. She tells him of a certain man, what he may or may not do with her, what she may or may not do to him, all this desire. He is back in his house, on the bed. He listens and thinks of how he loves her, if that how can be measured right, and what manner of love is in need of being measured.

The image of large water remains in his mind, this time from watching men who surfed on the Island, their bodies like songs. He tells his sister right then that one day she must see this, those men: I must return with you. Aww, you're sweet, she replies, and he begins to weep.

Sometime early the next morning, just as he wakes and picks up his phone, he reads an essay by a man who describes himself as "hopelessly optimistic." Not, in fact, the full essay. A short blurb in an email linked to the essay. He perceives he would carry those words in his mind, be interrupted in the middle of his banal day to check in on a mere phrase. Why optimism, why hopeless. Why qualify the future.

Now he has tightened his necktie and picked up his keys. Now he has turned the ignition, now he is pedaling gently. Now he is waving to a woman walking her boy to school. Now he arrives at a car park, now he climbs up the stairs. Now he stares at a blinking cursor, an Excel spreadsheet, and a beaucoup of numbers. Life is so. He sinks into banality.

On the Island, he sees a man singing to a tree. He has recalled that moment many times, and at no time does he feel in danger of hyperbole. Of course, a man sings to a tree, holding a lonely trunk in embrace. "May peace be multiplied to you, my friend, whether you go or stay." He does not dare interrupt the man, cannot dare put a languid word in that unerring image.

The day goes on. At the staff canteen he high-fives a coworker, then approaches an unoccupied table. His sister has sent a text, somehow hitting send thrice. "I want to see you. I want to see you. I want to see you." The light has gone off. In the darkened moment before the generator comes on, he sees the coworker he high-fived approach. He knows she will come with a question, and if he responds well, might tell a story.

One man in her story is Amadou in everything but name. He has devoted his adult life to one mission; incurious as far as money is concerned; loved by all but held in suspicion by those in power; never eager to dispel the half-truths attributed to him, however unsparing they may be. And so he is distracted when she comes full-circle with her tale, as if he has held on to a lifebuoy and missed the rescue ship. She slaps the back of his palm. "What's on your mind?"

He drives his coworker to her home, two streets away from his. Before she leaves the car she hugs him, saying take care, and he rests an awkward hand on her neck. She remains sitting and speaks of the feel of his hands. Lingering and hesitant, drawing close even if gradual, just enough for the tickle to turn warm. He replies that she makes too much of a small gesture. "I didn't touch you for long." She stares at him hard and sad. And he feels the knot in his lower back, like an intuition never tested.

His sister insists on sleeping over. She sings to him one of her songs in progress, humming provisional notes. It's almost complete, she says. Every time there is you in the lyrics she looks at the spot in his chest where there is a birthmark, where his unbidden anxieties thrives, or so she feels she imagines. He closes his eyes once the song is finished, and she sits beside him and holds his hand. In no other way could she prove her music as unfinished.

Why are you sad, his sister asks him, standing over the bed the next morning. There is a how, and a why. Of course he can say how, the lingering distaste for anything remotely promising to spark a smile. Why? Amadou had shown him the exact point in the water where he could dip a foot and get some warmth. Only a foot, better even a toe. At the moment they stood together it was proven and true. Never when he went there without Amadou. And why? And how, if he wishes, can he return? And what memory does the water hold of a body bruised and braised? He stirs from the bed and reaches towards her to pull him up.

How this. Not how long, how much, or how ever. Maybe how however. I don't want how as grammar or mere word. I want how for how, how for how much of love. How as how, how how. I want to place it in front of God, How God, how of expanse. I want how in repetition. How how. How how how. How.

Today he can bear it no longer. He seeks out his coworker as soon as he sees she is at her desk and asks if she has a moment. They stand in front of the stairs, and he places a firm hand on the rail. There, then, he tells her about Amadou. "He died." It is the first time he says this to anyone outside the Island. She says something to him. He'd heard, "How can I hold you?" But he doubts that. And once she brings him to herself, at first in a half embrace, and then with her hand on his nape, he wonders how to match what she might say or do with what he has seen or felt. "Hold me like this," he says.

All this desire. For, even before he left for the Island, when it was clear to him that, however repressed, his mind harbored affection for her, maybe lifelong, he hoped she would speak of those feelings first. She'd said, "I like us like this, complicated." He'd think nothing of it until now: in the time it takes for him to say more than a mere declaration. Yes, Amadou died. Now he must unknot that word for her, unfurl a main story of grief, not one where he is cast in one of several subplots.

He recalls a woman who sits beside him as the airplane leaves the Island. He pulls down the blind of the window. He despises the sensation of looking at the mottled world below. But she asks him if he can pull it back up, her tone near vicious, desperate. He obliges. Perhaps it is his hesitation—but she apologizes. "It is my first time flying. I am fifty-three, and I have never left this Island." He feels close to pity, if not solidarity. Would she mind if he sits where she sits, he asks? Would he mind, she asks? One view of the world is exchanged for another.

He has heard of all those regions of the world in which the sun stayed months without giving a shine. Intermediate light; light as potential. Amadou once said that to not dream must be the kindest form of torture: what do you do with all that darkness shut up in your eyes? He'd had no dream since his return.

His coworker insists on driving him home. In order to beat the traffic on Ikorodu Road, they must leave at sundown. With her hand on the knob, she looks at the sky. She says nothing about it and enters the car. He sees in her demeanor that gold, this expanse, how God. Now that he has told her of Amadou he hopes she might serve as counterpoint for his feelings. To reflect through her how the world goes on, shrugs off absence.

She insists on sleeping over. While she holds ajar his refrigerator, he weighs from the firmness in her voice how grave his loss seems for her and concludes there is no way to know—days from the Island lead here, days after the Island make a turn from here.

Synapses, Between

Lotte LS

Thereafter   there were shadows grazing the sugar granules
artificial limelight consoling every picture frame

swallows lived underground during winter

the trees work against themselves   splendid bitches
naïvely ironing their suits

looking forward to becoming a toddler two hundred years from now

when the person in the photograph   is I seven years from now
this spring   I grew half an inch

I will be gone before I is seven years from now   birthdays
of conkers sinking pockets

anniversaries
of expired feelings   laters, mwah

there is another world   but it is outside this one
when you spoke everything in the room just disappeared for me

when everything   how do we

what I found underneath was moss I took out my pocketknife
reluctant to abandon my dead   my one consolidating death

a part of   how it helped me to see

I don't mind g-o-d but I don't care for his groundsmen
the imperfect o   of their knees

o   I am so thankful for the seeing

Other People

Amanda DeMarco

There is a passage in the Analects where Confucius sighs, "No one knows me." In taking this quotation out of context, I am no doubt doing a disservice, but such aberrations exert a special fascination, as if civilization itself were declining to claim fellowship with the great family of woman, and wishing (in the affecting language of Mr. Wordsworth)—Humbly to express / a penitential loneliness. This notion made me feel that I was not separate and alone in my solitude. As a "creative person" I had grown accustomed to thinking of myself as a lonely wanderer contemplating a desolate scene, either a wintry landscape or a graveyard. The sternness of my habits of thought was forever in temptation of lapsing into infidelity by denying the insight that transcends the individual. For important social reasons, people like to think that other people are totally unlike them—but these differences are, in reality, for most functions, rather small. Let us put it this way: our collective culture is the medium through which people speak. And if you don't understand that, how can you say anything at all? How, I ask you, can I?

On Freud's desk he kept a statue of Asklepios, the god who loved human beings most. And maybe in the mind of our Creator where we whirl about as if in a millrace, we interpenetrate and are interpenetrated by fellow creatures by the thousands. A human being lives out not only her personal life as an individual, but also, consciously or subconsciously, the lives of her epoch and contemporaries. These identifications define a larger self, a map of affections and alliances, and the limits of this psychic self are nothing more or less than the limits of love. But I read Freud only for literary truths. Within the parameters of one's own realities, one must seek one's own answer or solution. Each person must, on some level, take herself as the calibration point for normalcy. Our own experiences feel necessarily more real than other people's.

In my case, books taught me about myself what mixed and erring humanity could not. The broad sweep of human social life revealed itself to me as a vast text, which lacks both notes and bibliography. The text speaks, that is all. Because this shared story is equally reflected in all parts of this universe, the difference between reading the world and living in it breaks down. Whoever reads it quickly understands that nothing ever ends, and there is especially no end to individual fictions, fictions created by individual human beings. They are like the stories God tells: full of impossibly particular information. The simple notion of reading as the revelation of a common past, a shared story, sent a wave of emotion over me. As if only by reading I again belonged to a race of human beings like myself.

In books, people open their doors, let you in, they answer questions about intimate parts of their lives. You imagine other people, and in whose world is the imaginary defined as that which is not real? Serious fiction's purpose is to have an oar in every woman's boat, to taste of every dish, and sip of every cup. To read, and read, and read still more is to specialize in humankind.The great works of art and philosophical constructions have remained uncomprehended not through their too great distance from the heart of human experience, but the opposite. This is what intensive reading is: a long road to travel before you arrive at human matters.

But what is that common experience? Culture is compatible with all kinds of horrors. Inheritors of this anxious paradise, votively we cluster in the dark, abandoning ourselves to rumor, translation, transcription, letter writing, note-taking, testifying, confessing, lying for personal gain, lying for sport. That is, an artistic activity, commentary upon the life and habits of the human race. Literature has consolidated itself, prospered, and become what it is—one of the hugest dimensions of mankind—to express and resolve, albeit magically, the contradictions which remain hidden or unresolved in the parent culture.

But however we may cry out for magic, it's not easy to set the soul spinning a web of dreams. Most of our platitudes notwithstanding, self-deception remains the most difficult deception. The illustrious magician Robert Houdin wrote a manual on conjuring whose eighth recommendation was: "Although everything said during a session may be, in a word, nothing but a web of lies, one must immerse oneself deeply enough into the spirit of one's role in order to believe oneself in the reality of the fables being uttered." This achieved, the human capacity for self-delusion is apparently infinite—which is nothing against it, for illusions are the most valuable and necessary of all things, and she who can create one is among the world's greatest benefactors. The test of a book (to a writer) is if it makes a space to rationalize, to explain, why one would keep returning, like Freud's grandson, with his *fort-da* game, to the same miserable scenario, the human condition.

In science fiction, humanity is often described as a collective, and in my youth it was easy for me to develop beautiful fantasies about such a civilization. This grandiose sublimity embracing the whole of humanity put me at home in my species. I cannot get by, in other words, without a pinch of pathos, since it is the utopian dream that drives me. She who stands aloof runs the risk of believing herself better than others, highlighting the insecurity of the very concept of individuality. To this way of thinking, the sovereignty of one's individuality is, I suppose, a reaction against the utopian dream, a kind of heroic despair or craven arrogance. But for language even to be possible, it must always be a *function of relationships between persons*. At a certain level we speak, and therefore write, like everyone else—in the text, the fade-out of voices is a good thing.

Maybe Freud loved people most, or more than most, or most likely he was one of the most curious people about other beings. We are brought up in the ethic that others, any others, all others, are by definition more interesting than ourselves, but I'm a native informant as well as a researcher. I imagine, in other words, that this book is about other people. But of course it is not. My project was to be an acute but non-interfering observer—a scribe, not a poet, and these pages contain other women's thoughts, but always my preferences, because unwillingly I participate in everything. As is so often the case, the intensity of our need to be understood distorts our positions, though our interest itself may still be complete and human.

As regards other people, as regards humankind or humanity, no, I do not believe I am cynical at all. Louis-Ferdinand Céline says: when you've reached the very end of all things, and sorrow itself no longer offers an answer, then you must return to the company of others, no matter who they are. (To say 'we' and mean 'I' is one of the most recondite insults.) I know this, yet it is a common occurrence in life that our behavior is in direct opposition to what we know. The myth of Oedipus can never be experienced as warning us not to get in an oedipal constellation but I am what you might call conflicted.

How did our sorrows come to be? We learn from Marx that 'Women make their own history, but they do not make it just as they please.' You cannot learn, through common sense, *how things are*: you can only discover *where they fit* into the existing scheme of things. The overwhelming power of custom, the limitations of human knowledge, the primacy of experience, the dangerous absurdity of fanatical belief, the vulgar pretensions of civilization, and the abiding truths of nature are just facts—or mysteries, if you like. Who would dare ask azure heaven to explain? As Petrarch observes, we change language, habits, laws, customs, manners, but not vices, not diseases. How mutable are our feelings, how recent are the notions that life should be "comfortable," that those who live it should be "happy."

We want our children to believe that, inherently, all women are good. But children know that *they* are not always good; and often, even when they are, they would prefer not to be. The human race is a naive species and every place is full of metamorphosed and two-legged asses. Who knows why people do what they do. Most people don't notice anything at all, or care, if they do. Women are so blind that they even take pride in their blindness. Some have held that snow is black, that the earth moves, that the soul is air, fire, water; but all this is philosophy. When falsehood can look so like the truth, who can assure themselves of certain happiness?

Worse, most people understand not the state of their own souls. People know what they want because they know what other people want. They express all the contradictions of the contemporary crowd: its opportunism, narcissism, desire for autonomy and creation, its inability to focus or make up its mind, its constant readiness for transgression and simultaneous submission, but they still feel an overwhelming, instinctual identification with their own species.[1] (Though Germans of a particular generation are still regarded as standing a little outside humanity and I doubt very much [trying hard to look back] whether young children really think of themselves as the same species as adults.) The unsalty, free flowing tears of the uncultured fuse together in a common teeth-gritting harmony.

Perhaps the lowest common denominators of our lives and consciousness are wholly expressed within the two lines: Though you hide behind a threshold of indestructible iron, / The mound shaped like a wheat-cake will claim you

---

[1] Or, if we turn the argument around, not being human is invariably a form of punishment. If a snake crawled up to you and said it would serve you, would your fear and disgust cease? There is a story by Franz Kafka—perhaps you know it—in which an ape, dressed up for the occasion, makes a speech to a learned society. And surely no one would be surprised to discover that Christ had dined that last evening with his disciples on the lamb he used as a trope for humanity.

for its own. Everyone dies. Thersites' body is as good as Ajax', when neither are alive. It is a horror of all shared experience, all shared being, all *genus*: a life span is nothing compared with death's eternity. Winnicott once accused Freud, for example, of using the concept of the death drive to "achieve a theoretical simplification that might be compared to the gradual elimination of detail in the technique of a sculptor like Michelangelo." You had only to keep asking about the value and meaning of the next smaller unit to realize that taken together they would not add up to a sum, but rather that such calculations led to diminishment, obliteration, shrinkage, and annihilation.

I had known that dying turns people into an incoherent jumble of meaningless forces that gets rolled round in earth's diurnal course like rocks and stones and trees, because I had read it in *The Education of Henry Adams.* And Freud rightfully said that whoever asks for the meaning of life is sick. From this it follows that she must be healed, not satisfied; and if not healed, then consoled. This forced me to consider the absurdity of learning about others as an affront to the mystery that is human action and the human heart. Confronted by problems which have puzzled the wisest of women, the truth may be that it offers nothing.

Yet, in candour, I will admit that the desire to solve riddles, to dismantle paradoxes is universal and timeless. If you show people slides of triangles, circles and squares in relation to each other, they will narrate stories about them chasing each other, running away, forming a crowd while a loner stands outside. This echoes a well-known story in which the ancient philosopher Zhuangzi and his friend Hui Shi look at the fish swimming in the water and hold a famous discussion about "whether one knows if the fish are happy." The interpretive ghost haunts people, even when we try to elude it: whether Sappho was a courtesan; whether the egg came first or the hen; and similar nonsense which, even if one had learnt it, ought to be forgotten. The human heart, with its questions and riddles, has a general bent for paradox. Fortunately, we are not forced to rely on random free association to teach us about ourselves. As all customs were founded upon some bottom of reason, they illustrate something deep in the grain, something unadmitted. For better or for worse, civilization is meant for us. Humanity has become herself her own Fate.

It takes long, arduous work, great knowledge of literature—but even more so life—to 'read' society with the requisite subtlety. In humanist jargon, the highest vocation of literature is to explain woman to woman. Nowadays I know the true reason I read is to feel less alone, to make a connection with a consciousness other than my own.

And while none of this will lighten life's burden, it gives us a continuity, something to return to, and offers a familiarity that allows some portion of our own lives to remain connected and coherent. At bottom, it's a theological exercise—the impressive act of those who believe they can unite in their person all possible human divisions and fragmentations. It is not absurd—is it?—to concern oneself with what people have in common rather than with what sets them apart.

Whatever point of the compass one follows, then, the overall point is clear: no woman is an island-ess. Each person must, on some level, settle down to a place if not in the sun then at least in the consensus. It is difficult to believe, is it not? (The subject wants to cede herself to the collective without being cancelled by it. Letting oneself go, in fact, is doubtless a definition of madness in many cases.) Even I am not sure, as I listen to my own voice. We are a company of fools, I am one of you—and if that is the case, how are we ever meant to know, except by existing in a state of absolute pessimism, our true level? Greater spirits than I were confounded with more than customary violence by the subject. Heraclitus the philosopher, out of a serious meditation of women's lives, fell a-weeping and with continual tears bewailed their misery, madness, and folly. Democritus, on the other side, burst out a-laughing, their whole life seemed to him so ridiculous.

SOURCES (IN ALPHABETICAL ORDER)

Hans Abendroth, *Null und Eins*;
Theodor Adorno, *Minima Moralia*;
Louis Althusser (quoted in Dick Hebdige *Subculture and the Meaning of Style*);
Antonin Artaud, *The Theater and Its Double*;
Saint Augustine, *Confessions of a Sinner*;
James Baldwin, '*Equal in Paris*' (in *Baldwin: Collected Essays*);
Roland Barthes, *A Lover's Discourse*;
Paul Beatty, *The Sellout*;
Lucia Berlin, *A Manual for Cleaning Women*;
Bruno Bettelheim, *The Uses of Enchantment*;
Hans Blumenberg, *Care Crosses the River*;
Thomas Browne, *Hydrotaphia*;
Thomas Browne, *Religio Medici*;
Robert Burton, *The Anatomy of Melancholy*;
A.S. Byatt, (in introduction to Thomas Mann's *The Magic Mountain*);
Zongqi Cai, 'Pentasyllabic Shi Poetry: The 'Nineteen Old Poems' (in Zongqi Cai [ed.], *How to Read Chinese Poetry—A Guided Anthology*);
Roger Caillois, *The Writing of Stones*;
J.M. Coetzee, *Elizabeth Costello*;
Phil Cohen (quoted in Dick Hebdige *Subculture and the Meaning of Style*);
Teju Cole, *Open City*;
Averill Curdy, *Song and Error*;
Rachel Cusk, *Outline*;
David Damrosch, *How to Read World Literature*;
Angela Davis, *An Autobiography*;
Thomas De Quincey, *Confessions of an English Opium-Eaters*;
Amanda DeMarco, '*The Island of Second Sight*' by Albert Vigoleis Thelen (on Three Percent; https://www.lit-across-frontiers.org/resources/three-percent);
Joan Didion (Quoted in Zadie Smith, *Changing My Mind*);
Joan Didion, *Slouching Towards Bethlehem*;
Jenny Diski, *What I Don't Know About Animals*;
John Donne (quoted in Alice Notley; quoted in Chris Kraus, *I Love Dick*);
Charles Egan, 'Recent-Style Shi Poetry: Quatrains (Jueju)' (in Zongqi Cai [ed.], *How to Read Chinese Poetry—A Guided Anthology*);
August Endell, *The Beauty of the Metropolis*;
Chengda Fan, 'Walk in the Cemetery' (quoted in Cao Xueqin, *The Story of the Stone*);
Paul Fleming (*translator's note* in Hans Blumenberg, *Care Crosses the River*);
Kate Flint (in introduction to Virginia Woolf, *The Waves*);
David Foster Wallace (quoted in Zadie Smith, *Changing My Mind*);
Goethe (quoted by George Eliot; quoted in Zadie Smith, *Changing My Mind*);
Stephen Greenblatt (in introduction to Thomas Browne, *Religio Medici*);
Stuart Hall (quoted in Dick Hebdige, *Subculture and the Meaning of Style*);

Dick Hebdige, *Subculture and the Meaning of Style*;
Franz Hessel, *Walking in Berlin*;
Wolfgang Hilbig, *The Sleep of the Righteous*;
Ben Hutchinson, *Comparative Literature: A Very Short Introduction*;
Holbrook Jackson, in introduction to the 1932 edition of Robert Burton, *The Anatomy of Melancholy*;
Franz Kafka, 'A Common Confusion' in *The Complete Stories*;
Franz Kafka, 'The Warden of the Tomb' in *The Complete Stories*;
Esther Kinsky, *River*;
Mary Kinzie, *Drift*;
László Krasznahorkai, in introduction to Wolfgang Hilbig, *Sleep of the Righteous*;
Chris Kraus, *I Love Dick*;
Rachel Kushner, *The Flamethrowers*;
Nathalie Léger, *Exposition*;
Nathalie Léger, *Suite for Barbara Loden*;
Xinda Lian, 'Ci Poetry: Long Song Lyrics (Manci)' (in Zongqi Cai [ed.], *How to Read Chinese Poetry—A Guided Anthology*);
Bu Lin, 'Lament for My Wife No. 3' (in Egan, Ronald. 'Shi Poetry: Ancient and Recent Styles' in Zongqi Cai [ed.], *How to Read Chinese Poetry*—Cixin Liu, *The Dark Forest*);
Cixin Liu, *The Three-Body Problem*;
Cixin Liu, *The Dark Forest*;
Thomas Mann, *The Magic Mountain*;
Michel de Montaigne, quoted in Robert Burton, *The Anatomy of Melancholy*;
Franco Moretti, *Distant Reading*;
Maggie Nelson, *The Argonauts*;
Yoko Ogawa, *Hotel Iris*;
Mary Ruefle, *Madness, Rack, and Honey*;
Phillip Schönthaler, *Portrait of the Manager as a Young Artist*;
William Shakespeare, *Cymbeline*;
Mary Shelley, *Frankenstein*;
Zadie Smith, *Changing My Mind*;
Zadie Smith, *White Teeth*;
Rebecca Solnit, *The Faraway Nearby*;
Susan Sontag, *Against Interpretation*;
Susan Sontag, *On Photography*;
Susan Sontag, *Under the Sign of Saturn*;
Hito Steyerl, *The Wretched of the Screen*;
Xiofei Tan, 'Pentasyllabic Shi Poetry: New Topics' (in Zongqi Cai [ed.], *How to Read Chinese Poetry—A Guided Anthology*);
Lynne Tillman, *Men and Apparitions*;
Simone Weil, *Gravity and Grace*;
Virginia Woolf, *A Writer's Diary*;
Virginia Woolf, *Orlando*;
Nell Zink, *The Wallcreeper*.

The Translation [The Metamorphosis *in multiple*]
Franz Kafka—*a translation of extant translations by* 0x0a

The Translation *is a piece of digitally aided poetry, which takes the first two paragraphs of seven translations of Franz Kafka's* **'Die Verwandlung'**—*usually translated* **'The Metamorphosis'**—*and runs them through a computer program that exchanges nouns, adjectives and verbs with a synonym. It thus multiplies the amount of Kafka translations in existence along the axis of synonyms within the same language rather than between languages.*

—**0x0a**, 2019

The Mutation

Translated from the English of **David Wyllie**

One morn, when Gregor Samsa woke up from troubled dreamings, he happened himself mutated in his berth into an atrocious varmint. He rested on his plate-like dorsum, and if he raised his caput a bit he could understand his brownish abdomen, slightly domed and split by arch-ways into starchy sectors. The bedclothes were hardly capable to spread over it and appeared quick to skid off any minute. His many branches, pitifully lean likened to the sizing of the remainder of him, beckoned about helplessly as he beheld.

"What's transpired to me?" he supposed. It wasn't a dreaming. His chamber, a right human chamber although a bit too little, rested peacefully between its four conversant barriers. An aggregation of fabric trials rested spreading out on the tabular array—Samsa was a roving salesman—and above it there dangled an image that he had recently reduced out of an illustrated mag and put up in a decent, gilded structure. It expressed a dame suited with a pelt chapeau and pelt feather boa who sat down upright, lifting a fleshy pelt fumble that spread over the unit of her lower branch towards the spectator.

The Transmogrification

Translated from the English of **Donna Freed**

As Gregor Samsa aroused from unsettling imaginings one morning time, he chanced himself transmogrified in his seam into a monstrous pest. He sat on his difficult armorlike rear and when he elevated his mind a slight he realized his overleapt chocolate-brown venter split up into subdivisions by buckram arches from whose tallness the coverlet had already tumbled and was about to slip off completely. His many ramifications, which were pathetically slender equated to the balance of his majority, wavered helplessly before his discernments.

"What has occurred to me?" he considered. It equalled no ambition. His elbow room, a veritable human sleeping room, if a slight minor, sat restrained between the four intimate parries. Above the bureau, on which an accumulation of cloth sample distributions was unpacked and diverged—Samsa was a tripping seller—hung the icon that he had recently scratched out of an explained fortnightly and sat in a pretty gilt human body. It exhibited a madam, sitting around upright, got dressed in a fur lid and fur boa; her full forearm had disappeared into a slurred fur muff which she kept out to the witness.

The Alteration

Translated from the English of **Ian Johnston**

One forenoon, as Gregor Samsa was awaking astir from anxious aspirations, he detected that in cradle he had altered into a scandalous verminous glitch. He was placed on his defence-hard stern and realized, as he boosted his brain up a fiddling, his dark-brown, condescending stomach separated up into stiff bow-like segments. From this acme the cover, just about ready to slue off entirely, could hardly remain in topographic point. His numerous pegs, pitifully sparse in comparing to the residual of his perimeter, flittered helplessly before his oculi.

'What's ensued to me,' he conceived. It constituted no aspiration. His scope, a proper scope for a mortal, only somewhat too modest, placed quietly between the four eminent ramparts. Above the mesa, on which an unpacked assemblage of specimen material goods was distributed (Samsa was an itinerant marketer) hung the likeness which he had extracted out of a demonstrated cartridge a fiddling while a gone and fixed in a sweet gilded scaffold. It was a likeness of an adult female with a hair cap and a hair boa. She modelled rigid there, getting up a stir in the guidance of the watcher a hearty hair botch into which her total forearm vanished.

The Conversion

Translated from the English of **Joyce Crick**

As Gregor Samsa awakened one dayspring from restless pipe dreams, he bumped himself translated into some sort of horrific vermin. He posed on his knockout, reinforcement-like vertebral, and if he brought up his psyche a footling, he could find his curved charred gut, dissevered by vault-moulded ridges, and domed so eminently that the bedcover, on the threshold of being cancelled, could hardly rest posed. His many wooden legs, miserably flimsy in assessment with his magnitude otherwise, fluttered dependently before his optics.

'What experiences went on to me?' he opined. It represented not a pipe dream. His cubicle, a proper, earthling's cubicle, rather too small-scale, posed peacefully between its four familiar bulwarks. Above the board, on which his compendium of knit trials were ranged—Samsa was a commercial-grade holidaymaker—there hung the painting he had freshly trimmed out from an elucidated arsenal and waxed in a pretty gilded soma. It presented a ma'am sedentary posing set up, attired in a fleece fedora and fleece boa, and bringing up an overweight fleece muff, which downed her limb right up to the elbow joint, towards the looker.

The Evolution
Translated from the English of **Willa** *and* **Edwin Muir**

As Gregor Samsa roused one dawn from nervous delusions, he encountered himself translated in his bed into a mammoth worm. He made up dwelling on his severe, as it were protection-plated, nether and when he rose his nous a Lilliputian he could visualize his cupola-like auburn paunch carved up into potent patronizing slices on the top side of which the bed comforter could hardly maintain in military position and was about to slither off utterly. His numerous bases, which were wretchedly fragile matched to the deposit of his mass, brandished helplessly before his senses.

"What has passed of to me?" he rumoured. It was no delusion. His lodging, an even human sleeping accommodation, only rather too pocket-sized, was hushed between the four recognizable stockades. Above the counter on which a solicitation of textile tasters was unpacked and ranged out—Samsa was a moneymaking tourist—was strung up the mental picture which he received recently pared down out of an exemplified journal and positioned into an appealing gilt build. It demonstrated a gentlewoman, with a fuzz detonator on and a fuzz tippet, posturing upright and maintaining out to the ogler an immense fuzz muff into which the whole of her prime had went away!

The Adjustment
Translated from the English of **Joachim Neugroschel**

One dawning, upon wakening from fomented hallucinations, Gregor Samsa observed himself, in his crib, adjusted into a lurid parasite. He put down on his arduous, cover-like posterior, and when arising his chief marginally, he could comprehend his bronzed, vaulted belly partitioned off by curving ridgelines, while on the upper side of it, the mantle, about to slide sour altogether, could barely take hold. His many stages, woefully tenuous related with his overall cinch, tripped the light fantastic helplessly before his watch.

"What has chanced me?" he inquired. It comprised no hallucination. His hall, a normal if somewhat bantam hominoid hall, spread quietly amongst the four memorable parapets. Above the slab, on which an argumentation of framework samples was unpacked and increased out (Samsa was a wayfaring clerk), hung the impression that he had recently nipped from a proven weekly and infixed in a comely gilt figure. The impression verified a noblewoman riding there vertically, bedizened in a down sou'wester and down boa, with her integral forearm flying inside a clayey down muff that she seized out toward the bystander.

The Translation

Translated from the English of **Richard Stokes**

When Gregor Samsa came alive one aurora from panicky reveries, he discovered himself converted in his bedstead into an immoral louse. He was lounging on his backbreakingly shell-like hind, and when he moved up his top dog a niggling, he could visualize his arena-shaped brunette organic structure, rung with reinforcing arcs, on upside of which the quilt, ready to skate right off, conserved its precarious clasp. His abundant members, pitifully squeaky in intercourse to the residuum of his volume, boogied ineffectually before his eagle eyes.

"What has befallen me?" he imagined. It subsisted not a reverie. His vastness, a normal though rather too trifling human vastness, reposed tranquilly between the four acquainted fortifications. Above the lectern, on which an appeal of rag mock-ups had been undid and positioned out—Samsa was a peripatetic administrator—swung the scene that he had recently slashed out of a slick and climbed in a handsome gilt physique. It established a peeress in a hide trilby and boa deskbound orthodox and propelling out to the attestant a cloggy hide muff into which her intact antebrachium evaporated.

Nacre

Hannah Williams

On their second date he serves her oysters, all sea-wind and whistle-sharp. He wears a blue shirt, his eyes like light straining through deep, dark water.

He takes a little knife, twists it in between the oyster's lips, jimmies it open. She's shocked—thoughts of white tablecloths and silver cutlery glinting in the sun undercut with the brute force of it, the wrestle of muscle against muscle. When it lies open on its shell she's a little upset: at its roughness, the primordial feathering around the edges, the fossil-spiral of the meat.

She's read about oysters, knows, for example, that there are many kinds, most inedible: true oysters, pearl oysters, thorny oysters, pilgrim oysters, saddle oysters, dimydarian oysters, windowpane oysters, whose translucent shells hang in chandeliers and star-shaped lamps. Based on the names alone, she likes the autumn-thicket feel of the thorny oyster and the sweet purity of the true. She knows of their three-chambered hearts, their colourless blood, the five litres of water they filter every hour. These facts make her think of the large grills in swimming pools, the vast whirlpools in reservoirs where the water drains away and out of sight. Sometimes she dreams of ocean trenches, of divers fading into pinpoints in the dark.

He takes a Riesling from the fridge, hands it to her like a newborn. It's April, unseasonably warm, the cliffs seen from the train already covered in cow parsley, hawthorn blossom. No wild garlic yet, but she thinks she smells the promise of it. She presses the bottle to her forehead, the insides of her elbows, her chest, drops of condensation running down her arms and down her top on to her breasts and her stomach. He watches her do this. She holds his gaze until he shakes his head slightly, turns to get glasses out of the cupboard. When she hands the wine back to him to pour, she notices his tight grip on the bottle, the places where his skin meets where the glass had touched her flesh. He toasts her; she drinks deeply.

When he squeezes lemon on it, she half expects it to shrink away. She puts three drops of Tabasco on it, like she read about when she Googled it earlier that day—a modest amount. It feels vaguely foolish, prescriptive, so she adds a little more, then worries about obscuring the taste. The lemon-and-sauce pool, red drifting through the liquid. She thinks of blood in the water, of tequila sunrises, of the looseness of alcohol moving through the body.

He says *drink it down! fast!*

There's something in the urgency in his voice that makes her feel as though something has become unstuck, nerve twanging loose. Like seeing the root of a tooth. She pours it back like a shot, mouth against the silted rim of the shell, the jagged edge keen against her lip. It slides back soft, easy against the lining of her throat, yet something else—lemon, Tabasco—sharp as a hangnail and full of the sea.

Things the oyster tastes of: the first glimpse of the sea from the train, nothing, the perfect spiral of whelk shells, sourness, splintering wood left on the shore, vinegar, wading at the sea's edge because the water is too cold, sand found in shoes weeks after going home, chili-heat. It tastes like the idea of the seaside—of describing the ocean without using the words 'wet' or 'vast' or 'water'.

She thinks of gulls, their wide-open beaks, the way they pour food down each other's throats. The violence of their desire.

He's smiling at her.

How was it? I'm jealous

I wish it were my first time again. You like?

She's irritated by the fact that he thinks her consumption of the oyster belongs to him. She'd mentioned it briefly on their first date. His face all mock-shock, comedic outrage: *I've got to change that then.* She wonders now if that was why he suggested they have them; so that he could collect it, weigh it up in his palm, polish it like pebbles he found on the beach. It'd be an anecdote he told to his friends—her ignorance, her hesitance. She wonders if he'd include the way she licked her lower lip after she swallowed it down, the smile that drifted over her lips, or whether he'd see these as extraneous details, a distraction from his part in the story. But she wants more—more of him, more of the oysters. She sweeps up the used quarters of lemon with the side of her palm.

It was good, yeah. I'd like another.

She finds them gone too fast—as soon as she swallows one she wants another. They don't talk much. He shucks, she eats. She knows he is watching her, the hungriness in her movements, the convulsive thrust of her throat that moves the oyster-flesh down her gullet. When it's his turn to pour the oysters into his mouth she looks him straight in the eye, and he fumbles, spilling the liquor down his fingers. He licks it with an urgency that pleases her.

When they've eaten them all—five each—she looks at the pile of discarded shells, pearlescent as moonlight on the countertop. She wishes she could keep them, thinks of storing gold earrings in them, filigree chains. She wants them as a memento, feels a strange pity for their beauty and their roughness. She feels strange asking him for them though, as if it would be too intimate of a question; as if he'd widen his eyes slightly, turn his head to the side and say something like *Sure... How come?* Or worse, pretend he'd understood, but tell it to somebody later, leaving a pause for them to laugh at the punchline. In the end, she doesn't say anything at all, except *they're gorgeous,* and points at the shells. At first, he doesn't realize what she's talking about, and when he does he only says *yeh,* stacks them on top of one another, throws them in the bin.

The Splendor & Effluence of the Motorway

Lauren de Sá Naylor

A scrap of paper twitching on the passenger seat bears inscriptions: A55, M56, M6 (toll), M40, digit-clusters appending proximity to locations on my cross-country adventure through North Wales, Chester, Birmingham and Oxfordshire. Each cluster intersects with a visual signifier: first, wind turbines emerging from a frothy haze hovering on the Irish sea; second, pylons like iron skeletal structures aligned in rows, and connected by convex power lines loom over the unnaturally wrought rural inland; third, the elegant sweep of grey tarmac synchronizes with automobile cruising, under low late summer light, at the M6 toll road. These locations on the map (a body-system) are glanced at or otherwise perceived in the periphery of this body, a technological, affective body, activating gliding propulsion. I'm chanting road names over and over like a prayer or linguistic amulets to bless my journey. I repeat, divining a route in haptic conjunction with the car and all of the devices to which I am growing accustomed, speaking to the splendor and effluence of the motorway.

*

Driving has inducted in me a new register of erotic mapping. Libidinal energy in conjunction with the matter of the machine discharges linearly, in a dasein with the road and its consciousness in transit. In the figure of the automobile a carapace and active occupant synthesise in mutual participation: fleshly body, metal exoskeleton and a fuzzy border between them. Steeped in spatio-temporal fluidity, I inside its "body," I am it—it is me—in a synchronic sense "I" am not there, being elsewhere in the flow. As described by Kristeva in relation to pregnancy, there is no maternal subjectivity as such: it happens without me.

*

Roads reconfigured as cartographic arteries have fluid trajectories because of the traffic flow. I am obsessed with the way human and non-human fit together, as well as the way they slip-up in the striving for a smooth, uninterrupted passage. In each invocation of my corpus enacting muscle-memory articulation we move, beyond, forward, are moved, be. The sweep of mechanised propulsion is as if an eroticised interlocutor rousing this body I have entered with the force of intimate tactility. The poetics of driving synchronises with an autoeroticism of differently constituted matter enjoined, being like orgonite, both organic and inorganic, and sublimated across bodies of tarmac, lanes of protocol, emotional trajectories. The self is reassembled in phenomena such as a conjugation of shafts of light, encircling the wheel with rigid then loose fingers, applying pressure to a pedal, announced from a flexing of the flank of a thigh, etc.

*

The body and machine are touching. Being *in the driver's seat*, at the wheel, feet poised in the vicinity of brake, clutch and accelerator pedals, pulleys and levers to be compressed and released in a symphony of contacts. To a dissolving of mind-body borders at the intersection of erotic/vehicular I yield, liquefied by sense-data. I am the moment in the same way I am the body; I am present in time and space but from above, my hands touching the steering wheel describing shapes and gestures. Conscious of fluidity between this seeing and being and revealing and the unseeing, the pure being, into magical, hypnotic futurity.

*

Driving engenders and engineers phenomenologies of interconnectedness, brought into being at the intersection of a materially contained self with a road that is open. Being both driver and driven; leading and being lead. Deliberate yet restrained force. The pressing of one body against another thing, imprinting. The drive, to interweave and to be-with. Compression, gripping and oscillation in my comportment are choreographies attuned to the libidinal and its litany of technical manoeuvres of the outer shell, where body and machine become one, where I pose as yielding, posing the possibility of fluidity. The urge to put this fleshly entity to use in activating some *out-of-body* potential, to be the organic technology sparking the dualistic-manufactured composite entity. The poetic rationality of motorways describes an aperture into potential-space: the body's purposiveness in situ in the car, mechanising via programmatic surges in limbs towards a particular pulley or lever, sliding into tandem with something other. The engineered slithering capillary-esque structure of motorways are like the circulatory system of a body and vehicles are like blood cells in veins rushing forthwith. The particular, haptic choreography of vehicles in this system in the service of uninterrupted *flow*. The avoidance of braking, signified by the red taillight and its inter-vehicular mimicry affect, is the paramount aim in pursuit of the maintenance of rhythm, the rise and fall of gears affecting speed, gentle halts and growing acceleration, appropriately. The driver's feet and hands are locked into a gentle routine of contacts with the levers of the machine, compressing and caressing, flesh and chassis, a synchromorophic rhythm of lustrous hardware peddled by soft bodies.

*

Easing down a tarmac and tree-lined chute, promising pacification or the glamourous Modernist dream of motoring and its associated liberations, of which the reality of a network of congested concrete arteries reliably falls short.

*

By-passing the tangled web of Birmingham traffic, the M6 toll road connotes a lux decadence in the very decision to exit onto it. Metaphors pertaining to residual intimacies are repurposed and accumulate intensity as I careen southbound on its glorious surface, feeling its sweep inside me and unperturbed by congestion or even the possibility of it, it is a magical catalyst of aural and sensational, addressing this body-in-pieces at an exact pitch.

*

The erroneous 'nature' of the body and the harsh 'manufactured' machine generating libidinal energy, originating in the lower part of my abdomen, echoing the viscerality of fight or flight that is corporeal-sexual. Any flavour of dominance is occluded by this streaming coherence of artificial binaries. Swelling being also tender, fragility entwines with a desire for its unending perpetuation. Whirling with a sublime sense and the libidinal sublimation of its affect: *I am my body, this car, the road; we are one cyclical entity.* The boundaries dissolve and in that moment of coming/melting I come into contact with a revelatory overwhelming of the sensorium, a coursing of energy the body through, a vortex in which motion, time and space meld. A constellation of affects plume, as how other orders of physicality enabling the quieting of mind and a tuning in to the sublime.

*

The transient happenstance of registering, tempered by the body's attentiveness to muscle ritual, creates a sense of ritualised process unfolding. Moments are multiply transient, building layers into a journey where space, time and motion coalesce. Temporally displaced from one moment to the next, over and over, I am re-constituted, somehow narcotised by, say, iridescent reflections bouncing back and forth from the sea to the shiny patina of the cars that pass mine, some glittering, others slick. A trinity of ochre, gold & blue make up the majority of the latter part of the drive, in which the sun has bowed down and the shadows have become achingly protracted across various tarmac road surfaces, and why not designate it 'holy'. Colours and hues daubing the outside penetrate the psyche by stealth in a fugue state of consciousness.

*

In these encounters with the self in its fragmentary resistance and desire, everything is already constellated and cohering. What happens in the car is marked by trace, always. It's the only place in which my desire is is never left wanting. There's no mirror, no interpolator into my stream of movement through matter and thought. The way that thought prickles and shakes and moves in tandem with vehicular motion in which my body is yet motionless, all under the mark of eros, the libidinal articulation of lack and within the arc of desire.

*

The poetics of automobile transit: vibrating particles in a frictionless cell; scraping open a fresh gape; to have a warm, flowing, transience seizure. Something sharp and pointed but soft and admissible, softness pronounced by the solitudinal and the motive. Dreaming, awake, dreamy scenography of actualised sublime, tonally, sensually surging outwards, discharge, libidinal, sluicing. This libidinal cathexis, attachment, clinging, is overdetermined by the music I play over and over, repeatedly. I flick the stereo switch agitatedly to repeat excised sections of sound, twisting the dial to max until the interior bulges with sound.

*

I've got Shikuza's 天界のペルソナ (*Heavenly Persona*) blasting in my Honda Jazz—it's my first car and some of the finest noise I know. There's something percolating in the rush of sound and motorway driving; her illegible lyrics seem to rise up out of earthly sludge with embroidered solo guitar throbs that tease, memory-relapse folds into momentary melancholy. Drowned sorrow and a crescendo verging on orgasmic as the M6 toll highway curves, bending as if a stalk into the lowering sun's long shadows, in a trance-state. Aural licks that curl about my driving body, being also guided into a multi-sensory overture: jouisssance!

*

Blue sky is dappled with cotton-wool clouds when I sweep into the M6 toll services. I park some distance from the other cars (why would I flock with a crowd when I have mastered my own space?), I fling open the car door in the manner of a stable gate having sequestered some wild animal; I roll-up and light a cigarette, capturing with each inhalation a rare feeling of corporeal fearlessness in my intoxicated lungs. I am breathing in light and utterly satisfied, coming down from a gold and green-tinged submergence.

*

Lurking at the perimeter of a manicured picnic area in which clusters of bodies bask in the late afternoon sun's luminous rays, I ache with fervour/feverish panic/excitement. Rendered defenceless by the electronic sliding doors, I fail to engage with this zonal entry port, this threshold across which the quiescence to social and experiential encounters weigh heavy, and I steal myself there for a time. In lieu of my carapace or protective husk, in spite of being vastly safer removed from the car, I perceive a heightened vulnerability. The transfer from automobile interior to no-place services complex generates in me a feeling weightlessness and edglessness. I display, to myself, in myself, a naked susceptibility previously veiled by the car's faithful performance of impenetrability and the blind faith in its unimpeded continuation.

*

It is impossible to drift, disaffected, through this service station forecourt, demonstrated by the anxious mark over each of us as we stand in line for pissy coffee and hot pisses that spring urgently out of urethrae in WC's bisected by double-sided walls of mirrors. I face it proper in the multiple personae of my peri-reflected image ascending and descending simultaneously into a two-pointed oblivion. The hand basins are fortified by vases filled with astounding bunches of cut flowers, fresh flowers cut through the clinicality of the scene, for which my involuntary complicity is grateful. This is my desire, this prism being poetry. It is coming through me because of hypnosis and the low Autumn sun burnishing the afternoon with a specific luminescence, the smooth road and the curated music and the corporeal uncertainty and violent banality of glass and steel and manicured land. I can touch with the world through this prism, I can see it with my senses anew, my cells and my dreams. Hypnosis is "the coming of sleep," an "artificially induced condition" of leaving the body. I'm becoming external, internal. The poetics of a motorway service station is a poetics of uncertainty, the border-space, the undecidable, gestation and lack. It is airport-lite, transience seized in a cathedral that beckons one to indulge in the poorest quality of capitalist reality, all looked over by unloving CCTV and in view of the heavens above, dappled clouds visible through the vaulted ceiling, and I wonder how it sounds when the rains come down hard onto its repellent surfaces.

*

The indelible trace of a journey's colour persists and retroactive narrativization holds it closer. Colour, interlinking with light, with motion, with soil, with Oxfordshire, my car, my body, the sky, the ground [the tarmac, concrete, flagstones, gravel and my feet, bare, sheathed in leather or plastic, wounded or dancing], in a web or weave that perpetually expands, which means perpetually contracts: pulse, pulse. A pink with which I am already accustomed generating more intimate knowledge: the pink that enshrouds my sleeping body and, daubed on the old landing wall, bisected the first floor of my last home. It shows itself on the lowest clouds at sunset and saturates failed photographs. There's a lilac too, that of North Yorkshire late-summer heather, inseparable from driving though I never followed a thought through to a text on those childhood seizures; this lilac feels to me like the voice of Gillian Welch—low, murky, hopeless and sublime. Driving my daughter across that swerving moorland highway in late August, my hands sweaty on the wheel, fearful of speed and the swerve of a high, turbulent A road—divested of the rigorous protocol of the motorway with which I so readily symphonise. My entire body racked with libidinal misapprehensions, sensing the bifurcation of this landscape's Roman roads and fortuitous heather as the closest experience of the conjunction of home and death.

*

At Oxfordshire, tilled earth of the M40 hillsides beneath low, diffused sunlight is the same shade of cameo pink as a bygone artificial rose. Bright burning sphere, water vapour hanging in the ether, industrial aluminium, steel, glass, smoke plumes. Pastoral hypnosis of the visual sense and the traumatic beauty—the *religiosity*—of splicing through it at seventy. My senses are aroused by the eros and ego of driving, plus the epic gloriosity of the M6 toll road: majestic curvature punctuated by vehicles moving at pace inside space, majestic beneath low-slung late autumn sunshine, iridescent steel and glass.

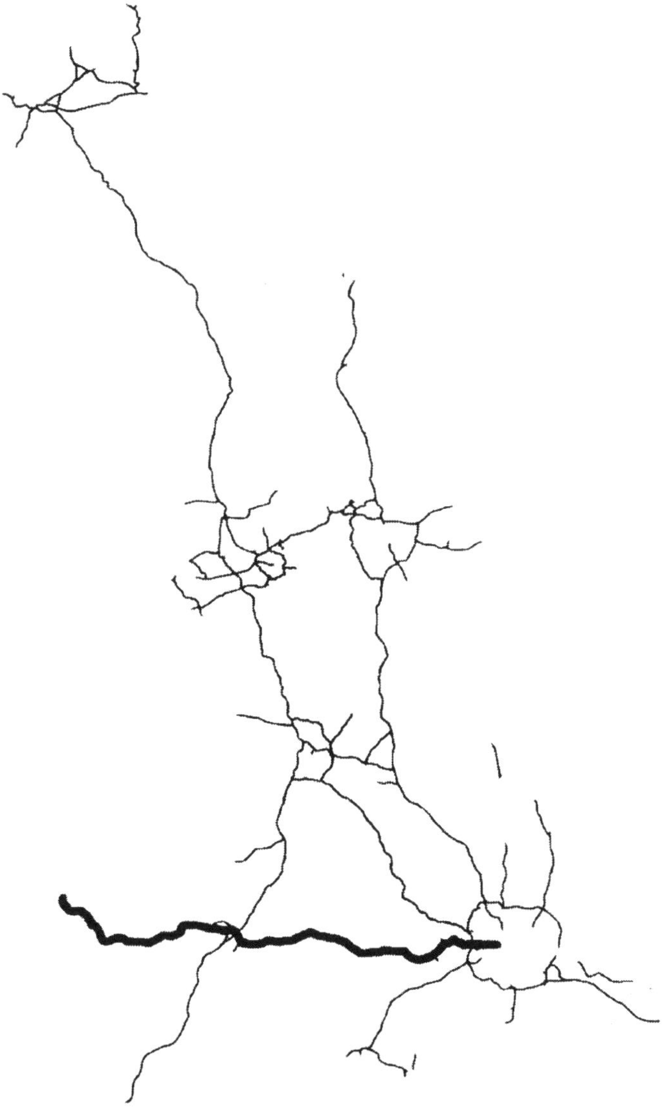

A Questionnaire—*An excerpt from a work-in-progress called* **Islets**

Jen Calleja

Examination on Critical Reading, Intimidation and Power Struggle

Q1

Close Reading of: —

This page of Wordsworth's diary
These two pages from a lawyer's appointment book
This love poem written by a bride the day before her wedding
This shopping list
These video rental receipts
This library card history
This desk rubbing
The changes made in this document
This lottery ticket
This advertisement
This job description
This curriculum vitae
The message in this birthday card

Answer:

Charles, the time spent under you has been invaluable to me. You came into my life when I was at my weakest. Separated from my husband, homeless after years on the road ruining my hearing, haggard for my age, fluent in a variety of tongues, fluent in the uses of a tongue. Endless wasted potential. Destiny brought me that newspaper, and the advert within it. I answered your call, and you answered mine. I'll never forget your fourth visit to the shelter, it was outside of visiting hours, I snuck you in. You bathed me, brushed my hair, tested my Dutch vocabulary, tucked me in.

Q2

Someone has been having doubts about an important part of their life, what could you say to get them to tell you more?

Answer:

You saw my innate potential and revealed it to me. For years I had believed that love was a wholly natural occurrence, rather than a phenomenon that requires acting with intention. You taught me how I have the capacity to make my dreams come true, and those of others, if I so wish. You taught me how I can change and penetrate the world around me to my advantage, without anyone even knowing my hand was in it. How to win an argument, how to cause a riot. How to influence opinion, how to translate for certain ends. That to control the narrative is to control reality, that words and texts are magic.

Q3

Someone tells you that they feel powerful. What could you say or do to disempower them?

Answer:

I hadn't fully comprehended why I could invoke such reactions, behaviours, strength of emotion. Of all the lovers I have had in all those countries, cities, towns, villages, bars and basements, I believed they all wanted me for either my blank, naïve nothingness, or my absolute core, which they could see but I could not. I could see, now, that I am many people, and I was a different person to all of them, just as I saw something in them that I used as a crux, a key. One thing was certain: I am and always was an erotic being. Before you, Charles, I did not know!

Q4

What key things could you say to make a person doubt
a) their intelligence
b) their attractiveness
c) their perspective on something
d) their grip on reality

Answer:

That this was all inherently a part of me! That I was born this way, and born to be treated a certain way!

Q5

How will someone indicate that they want to open up to you?

Answer:

That they were like a set of instructions written upon me! Ones that others could read as soon as they saw me!

Q6

How do you lay the foundations for someone to fall in love with you?
(3-month campaign)
How do you lay the foundations for someone to fall in love with you?
(1-month campaign)
How do you lay the foundations for someone to fall in love with you?
(1-night campaign)

Answer:

That I am, in essence, provocative. Whatever pose I make, whatever words I speak, I cannot help but illicit attraction and curiosity in people. It's not my fault, and it's not their fault. To ignore it would be to deny myself my greatest power and deny the world the opportunity to experience it.

Q7

How can you replace an idea in someone's mind with your own idea?

Answer:

I learned how to trade with a currency I didn't know I possessed riches in. I had got only so far living off of the desires of others, or rather, allowing them to live their desires through me, but now I could be the one in charge of these transactions. I didn't have to only wait for them to come to me, I could approach, and make the most of those approaching me. Instead of having my funds drained, I could build up my fortune.

Q8

How do you signal to someone without words that you want to talk to them?

Answer:

You held me close to you throughout my disorientation. You warned me off answering questions from others regarding who I was. These were only distractions. Was I a boy or a girl? How old was I? Where was I from? Were my skin and hair my natural colour? Where had I been? You encouraged me to change my appearance, and to do so frequently. You would be my anchor through this turbulence until I became used to pivoting on the axis of my self. You were honest with me always. I no longer needed to look in mirrors. You became the only mirror I needed.

Q9

How can you convince someone that you're their…
a) equal
b) superior
c) lesser

Answer:

I could not have foreseen what would grow between us as collaborative peers and lovers. You made me work hard, and became like family to me. You took the place of my friends, my parents, my brother, all of whom I am estranged from and to whom I have little connection or anything in common. You set up arrangements with other students, those you had vetted, so I could test my body often and ward off romantic feelings for anyone, including you. (This latter part was one of my greatest challenges. Did I succeed?).

Q10

What English-language indicators can you use to make someone believe that you can speak no other languages?

Answer:

I have you to thank for everything. For taking me out of the shelter, for my scholarship to the Institute, for building up my resistance to romance and love and pain, slowly, over time.

Q11

How can you convince someone to buy you a drink and make them think that it was their idea?

Answer:

You made me understand that the world is a cruel place and that in order to survive you must use the weaknesses of others against them, as they would do to you. It's not simply a matter of getting pleasure from someone: if it's a matter of life and death, you need to use whatever you have to hand. A matter of life and death is, of course, subjective. But take Boyd, for instance. Part of me is intrigued by him, and he with me. On the surface he seems obviously weak. I could take him, and it might even be fun. Is that a good enough reason to destroy someone? Maybe not. But there's something about him that tells me that if I work on him, or even if I don't, my life is going to be affected forever, either now or later. I am damned if I do, damned if I don't. It's a premonition. Do I get to him, before he gets to me? There's something about him that makes me feel like we're locked into one another.

Q12

Listen to recording One. What are the couple upstairs arguing about?

Answer:

I know you dislike my interest in Boyd. I know you have forbidden me from approaching him. But you taught me to challenge myself. You probably taught him the same. I had been so naïve. But I have changed. Become as hard as stone, and as fluid as water. I exist in a void of every culture and society and ideology, I am ahistorical, I am quantum. I can be whoever you want me to be. This is a skill, as you would say.

Q13

Why is the man at the bus stop smiling in this picture?

Answer:

But there is still a doubt within me. And a fear persists, even beneath this strength. I have a fear that you too are just like all the others. That you are using a weakness in me that only you can see. That in order to be at my strongest, I need to also do battle with you. Bring you to your knees, if I truly am ready. I have realised that I don't know what your weakness is. And I know how to find everyone's weakness. If I can't solve you, then my training has been a failure. Surely.

Q14

Based on this person's shopping basket, how would they react in a dangerous situation?

Answer:

Perhaps I need to once more become the person my parents know and love. Or at least a version of that person. Ultimately, I am still haunted by being able to see the mystery in everyone, while remaining unable to see what people see in me. I am shrouded in mystery—a positive, you might say. But this leaves me as being no-one. I am asked euphemistic questions, and I wish someone would just ask me what they want to ask. Maybe out of these questions I would be able to answer the question of who I am. I know you've tried to show me with your words and actions. Perhaps I must take a quest to further understand what others see.

Q15

Based on this person's list of favourite pastimes, guess their telegram password. (*You have three guesses*)

Answer:

Maybe once my training has come to an end I should help keep my parents safe and secure, finally take some responsibility, not run away, make them feel at peace? Or maybe I should leave all this altogether and try a different path, once more alone. I know I said that I was interested in continuing to help with your work, to accept the postgraduate position, accept the Isletese mission you worked so hard to get for me, but, I have a question for you, Charles—will you let me go instead?

Five Poems—**A Public Mural** & **The Truckdriver** & **Malverde**
Cass McCombs

A Public Mural

Emma Goldman dance of the hippopotamus to rattle open the prison gate.
Mahatma Gandhi yarn-spinning to liberate the inner state.
Frantz Fanon from behind a white mask, the third world knows.
José Martí from behind a white rose, an apostle grows.
Dolores Huerta beaten by sfpd but her stockton stock was too tough.
Lolita Lebrón coming not to kill but die for love.
Archbishop Romero eucharist bullets for the poor's pastor.
Pancho Villa cockroach's triumph over the schoolmaster.
Martin Luther King the voice that can carry.
Patrice Lumumba freely elected by african dignity.
Augusto César Sandino reign of the spirit of light and truth.
Leila Khaled terror of exodus on the spirit of youth.
Sitting Bull mystery and humor across native land.
Malcolm X completing the hajj across saudi sand.
Nelson Mandela harmonious spear of the nation.
Zofia Yamaika one armed teenager vs. nazi suffocation.
Frida Kahlo hoping never to return to this lonely place.
Maurice Bishop the airport at the end of the rat race.
Souha Bechara aerobics instructor turned assassin.
Che Guevara beloved buddy and hungry argentinian.
Rachel Corrie standing alone for another's home.
Leonard Peltier doing time for the unknown.
Audre Lorde inequality upon the axes of identity.
Edward Said identity upon the falsehoods of oriental pity.
Aristide haiti's heart exiled to a revolving glass door.
Farabundo Martí one of thirty thousand lost at la matanza of el salvador.
Rigoberta Menchú an uprooted maya testimonial.
Cesar Chavez striking the farm, striking a deal.
Judi Bari in the shadow of the big tree.
Harriet Tubman killing the snake by night for hundreds free.
Assata Shakur now there's guns on both sides.
Madame Bình revolution means nothing if not happiness provides.
Emiliano Zapata the general's genderless ranks.
Marilyn Buck prison dreams of pulverized capital from black-owned banks.
Rosa Luxemburg the rich rubbed her out, may she rest in peace.
Joe Hill nothing like a song for the spirit's release.
Mumia Abu-Jamal along with his brother, refusing defense.
Bernadette Devlin the troubles bullhorn talking sense.

The Truck Driver and Malverde

On the mountains I was driving
a gigantic truck filled with traps
to rob the rich northerners
and return the loot to Sinaloa
where my mother was born

Straight heading to San Antonio
but first to be questioned
by a checkpoint puppet goverment
they too are criminals, but for the rich
in collusion with the Americans

They are waving my truck into the blockade
thinking they are so sexual
with their weapons outside their clothes
I also have guns, but not so foolish as to reveal
until it is my advantage to do so

As I approached the checkpoint, I was not scared
for around my neck was
an image of Jesús Malverde
surrounded by embroidered cardboard
I gave me a kiss and said a prayer
to protect me and my burden:

Malverde, I humbly ask a favor, spirit
(I placed a stone on his altar in Culiacán)
today I need your guide
to pass through this checkpoint
and deliver my burden to San Antonio

Malverde, who took from the rich
and delivered to the poor!
that has the same name as the Messiah
take care of me for a few minutes
and I will forever honor you

My truck came to an abrupt stop
the man with the gun asked my destination
San Antonio, because I do not need to lie
the man looked at me coldly in the eye
and he waved his hand at me to proceed

Malverde, blessed Saint of Sinaloa!
I kiss your image again!
and pray your spirit finds rest
on the other side of the legendary borderline
between evil and green

Dreamy Idiotic Visions of the Future

Rachel Genn

Three, four Winters ago I squished mistletoe berries on an apple tree in the garden
48 Retweets—339 Likes

Three or four years ago this tweeter squished mistletoe berries into the apple tree in her garden. Metaphors can stimulate us long before they are understood.

I chose the image for a presentation to show how writers can nourish other writers who seem nothing like them. The mistletoe looked such a cheeky, healthy, plump imposter. *You have no right to be there* I thought, at the same time as, *That's me.*

I used it to illustrate my relationship with Nobel-prize-winning oral historian Svetlana Alexievich, though I did not google whether mistletoe is a parasite on the apple tree or is simply an epiphyte (*living upon*) the apple tree, noting "There are those who will bet on fact to knock out fiction every time, but history is not shapely. It is not always fit. Fact and fiction are sometimes forced to rely on each other's mercy."

Is the mistletoe thriving on its opposite?

How did my berries get squished into Svetlana and what might they dare to become?

The mistletoe sits on the bough as something undreamed of. At the end of *Boys in Zinc*—Alexievich's response to Russia's chaotic and disastrous involvement in Afghanistan—there is an account of the civil lawsuit against her for making public the stories of those affected. Her counter statement reads: '... Send a mother a zinc coffin, and then persuade her to sue the writer who wrote how she couldn't even kiss her son one last time and how she washed the zinc coffin with herbs and stroked it....' Like the voices from *Second-Hand Time*, does the mistletoe seem wondrous *precisely because* it springs from that which seems not survivable?

I begin casting about for love whenever there's a crisis and often, crises start when I don't know how I will say what I've got to say next. It's possible that muses are no more than catalysts for a new relationship with your work: I have wondered whether muses are beckoned into being solely by the work yet to do. It gets me thinking: anyone who worships you is using you. You're not the end point for anyone's current. If the current is the real thing, you cannot be. I don't think that the mistletoe is the end of all of this.

After having kids, I pined for what the artist Jenny Eden calls 'sustained togetherness' with my writing. With one daughter in a pram and one in a sling, I traipsed between public space and baby group while truffling for the difficulty formerly afforded me by writing (not *this* kind of difficulty; not *this* 'sustained togetherness'). In the City Library I picked up a leaflet for the Chernobyl Children's lifeline. Host a child it said. Could I provide an immune system boost for children from contaminated lands.

Sasha would be with us by the August of 2013.

Mick was the charity coordinator and a Derby City Fan who called the interpreter from Belarus, Yorna. Before the kids arrived, he organised a fundraiser at a church in a miserable dip at Heeley Green in Sheffield. The guest of honour was to be a firefighter who had been forced to tunnel under the melting fourth reactor at Chernobyl to line it with concrete. When our guest arrived the church smelled of tupperware and was so dark it felt charred. The electric lights brought the ruin too much to life so we turned them off. '*Welcome*' We said. He showed us his bottles of medicines and we discovered in detail through his translator how he had helped build the sarcophagus around the reactor. Up close, we saw eyes repurposed not to see but to *go through* life this side of the blast. The formality of his moustache and his uniform seemed staged. His belief in our understanding was not evident, equally insufficient, the sympathy we were capable of. There wasn't a whiff of holiness to the church.

Mick streamed a black and white video of the first hours of the disaster from YouTube, where a helicopter, hovering above the reactor clipped an antennae and dropped like a stone into the radioactive pyre. Mick nodded; this was my cue to read from *Voices from Chernobyl.*

This was my introduction to Svetlana. I chose to read Monologue About a Whole Life Written Down on Doors. After the blast, inhabitants of Pripyat weren't allowed to take any belongings, but one man insisted on taking his apartment door. His whole family's measurements were on that door. The man's father had lain dead on the door, though no-one knew whose tradition this was. It became the door his daughter lay on it while she waited for her 'small coffin—like a box for a large doll.'

The man took the door through the woods at night. On a motorcycle. He said of the death of his daughter and those like her, 'When I talk about it, I have this feeling, my heart tells me—you're betraying them. Because I need to describe it like I'm a stranger.' Svetlana gives her subjects the room to work out their role in the plot of their lives, often giving voice to that which cannot be borne alone. Hearing other people's stories is holding a space open for what happened to re-enter. The Belgian filmmaker Chantal Ackerman says anything that is framed becomes fiction.

The church stands in the blast zone of my childhood. In remembering the church and where it is, somehow the ground remembers me and pulls me up the hill back to events that I haven't recalled because they warned me not to.

We used to play on wasteland called the Piggeries. At its edge, under a dome of withies was a den. Boys called Kerry, Shawbags and Alan Ray whose hair was cut by their fathers took me there. All of us were expert flobbers. One of them had a sloping fringe, as smooth and fine as paper but he spoke like a Toddler. You get in there.

It was summer, and the floor of the den was brittle with pages of porn mags. I pulled the withies apart then stepped inside while they looked in through the struts. Once I was at the centre they knelt and set the edges alight guessing what I would do. Watching the fannies and spread arses gobbled up by flame, I froze. Somebody's tits survived in a ring of black ash. Svetlana claims 'from the point of view of art, the butcher and the victim are equal as people.'

My horror was not at their indifference to my life but in the speed with which I snuffed out the flame of my outrage. Something I still have to do so that I don't burn to death.

Svetlana also says forgetting is a form of lying.

Care is creative attention. When remembering threatens to annihilate the subject, the listener helps bear the tension of the question without an answer. Her surfeit of care is in her craft, her orchestration of voices that alone might stand shocked at themselves for existing. In *Second-Hand Time* there are those cursed for trading their noble dream of a common future 'for rags'—we discover women on fire with sorrow, rage, women with meteoric force like this rare capitalist. 'Moscow!' the woman cries, 'I've always seen her as a competitor, from the moment I got there, she inspired a sporting rage in me.' The female voices that Alexievich collects affect me in a visceral way, making me know I can make *this happen*. Their struggles, alongside cherished predictions of possibilities, unleash a supernatural energy into the work—a surplus that powers readers and opens up the conduits via which writers find and communicate with each other. Sasha came to Sheffield from outside Minsk which was still in the zone of contamination in August 2013. On our doorstep, we were told that Sasha had removed his own eye with a knife while trying to open a can. During his stay he would be fitted for a prosthetic one. We were instructed to give potatoes at breakfast to our boy. The hole was not new but it was puckered and gave him a defeated look in his shoulders. He treated my daughters aged 3 and 6 as invisible. Kids won't shut up about holes where eyes should be. We bought him a helicopter drone, which delighted him, I think.

The charity made sure the whole of August was filled, every day an activity. South Yorks fire service decided these kids who couldn't listen were never going to understand how difficult a hose was to handle. We caused a pile-up on the Monsal trail forcing a local child off the disused rail track, tyres yabbering to a stop in the rough. Dentists visits were planned, even a trip to the seaside.

Imagine never having seen the sea. Then imagine that your first glimpse of it was to be Cleethorpes at low tide. Through one eye. Then imagine you don't get that glimpse because you have to have your new eye fitted on that day. Alexievich admits to asking herself a countless number of times—how is it possible to make it through the midst of evil without increasing the evil in the world?

'What am I obliged to defend?' she pleads in court, insisting, 'I do not use conjecture... I collect details and feelings, not only from an individual human life, but out of the air of the time, its spaces and its voices.... I gather the book out of reality itself.'

Of the woman in *Second-Hand Time* who leaves her husband and children for the prison lifer from her dreams, the villagers say, 'Something is percolating inside her... she wants everything at once.'

Alexievich's mix of journalism and reportage does not demean or diminish opposing desires of everyday women, even when they are framed within the dominant ideology as dreamy idiotic visions of the future. Despite the villagers, the woman's husband understood her, 'We all loved our Mama. She was always cheerful. She played the piano—she'd gone to music school and she sang. Made up fairy tales. For a little while, we had a TV, someone had given it to us as a present. The kids got sucked into the screen, it was impossible to tear them away, and it made them kind of aggressive, they started acting like strangers. So she went and poured water in it like it was an aquarium. The TV burnt out. 'Children go look at the flowers and trees instead. And talk to your mother and father.' Our kids didn't even get upset because Mama had said so....'

Sometimes, her subject's loquacity makes them seem free to ignore what has happened to them but she also waits for eloquence created out of pain. Abjection can speak, and expertly orchestrated, it does so in harmonies of devotion and lament. The past is still ahead of us, Alexievich warns as we readers wonder what will be the food for those who were starving for a capitalism they had never tasted?

Care is not emotional volume. When it comes to curating content, one cannot care enough about any of her subjects—Chernobyl, kidnap, beastings, protracted hardship, words trying to escape burned mouths sealed shut in Afghanistan. Hard Labour.

Her super-fit eye is still human jelly, her ear fleshy yet. Her devotion to what happened purifies the reading experience as if her surfeit of care has burned off any excess empathy that may get in the way of the unique contribution of each message to the whole work. When *Second-Hand Time* draws to a close, you realise the weight that has built in tissues of tales, and suddenly it is a book to press flowers in, ending with an old woman wondering what her life has been for: 'Have you seen my lilacs? I go out at night to look at them—they glow. I'll just stand there admiring them. Here, let me cut you a bouquet....'

I named my current project *Bouquet* in deference to Alexievich with the idea of capturing the wild variousness of myself and my own bound-while-dying siblings. I don't yet know how to tackle something I care so much about but don't want to be told what to be bothered by. I am waiting now for what am I bothered by to find me. In readiness, I think about the rebound of flora and the wolves returning to the landscape in the years since Chernobyl and, having heard that in the woodlands surrounding Pripyat, the feathery limbs of immense trees grow out through the empty tower blocks, I search out drone footage. The sublime territory that Alexievich has mapped for us will help us navigate our own.

The Automatic Tour Guide
Emmanuelle Pagano, *translated by* Sophie Lewis & Jennifier Higgins

I'm waiting for the automatic tour guide to die.

It would be a blessed release, to tell the truth. For us and for him. It pains me to see him now. He's not as popular as he was in the old days, when tourists used to come just for him, for the guide, and the *gîte* was booked up months or even a couple of years in advance.

He isn't a guide, he's more of a storyteller, an automatic storyteller. Perhaps we should have called him the automatic raconteur, but because he's sometimes more like a geographer-geologist-historian or a guide for armchair hikers, pointing out the paths his stories take, we've always called him the automatic tour guide.

His name is actually Ukalo.

It's January and the lady from social services keeps going on at me. We won't be able to leave him where he is for another whole winter or they'll come and put him in a home. Still, I'm not that worried, because I'd be surprised if he lasts much longer, what with all the trouble we had with him last winter and him refusing to leave the shelter. If only he'd let us do it up a bit, build proper walls, insulate it or something, but he's stubborn, like all the old people from these parts, even though he isn't really. I mean he isn't really from these parts. He's definitely old. And stubborn. Won't admit he can't look after himself anymore, so we just have to watch him fading away and wait for him to drop down dead.

Better to have him drop dead here than put him in a home.

I take his lunch every day. He goes home and waits for my Tupperware.
In the evening he manages by himself, making soups with vegetables from the garden or from tins. It gives him something to do until the news comes on.

The *gîte* isn't like it used to be and we often get people who don't know about him. They don't come for the automatic guide, they come for the drama of the panoramic views, or just for the shrill, brutal air of the plateau, for the blue-shadowed snow on very cold days, for the autumn blaze of the maples, the great daubs of green in summer. Some end up in the area more or less by chance and the tourist office sends them along without warning them.

They're surprised, that's for sure, and sometimes taken aback.

This week's guests haven't opened the back door once and they're leaving soon, before midday. Ukalo is taking it badly. He hasn't said anything but his silence is hard to bear and I've been worrying all week, wondering whether they were going to open the door or not. They're packing their bags now, going back and forth dirtying the snow with their feet, loading their stuff into the squeaky-clean 4x4.

This whole week I've kept an eye out, not making it too obvious and not hanging around too long either, because it's bloody freezing. I've seen Ukalo sitting so close to the fire he could have burned himself, poking the embers with his battered stick, crushed by the waiting. I think he's been going over all the tales and legends in that leaky head of his, to pass the time and improve his performances, and to compensate a bit for the sudden memory lapses. It's perfectly normal, given his age, but for an automatic guide it's a blow. He invites us over to have coffee with him nearly every day, and when he goes blank in front of us, when he opens the door and forgets why we're there, I see him disappear from behind his face, and that wrinkled face is like a fallow field, useless.

Sometimes he makes it into a joke, and with the imagination he's got, he comes out with all sorts of funny reasons for it. Bizarre excuses for the gaps in his memory. Oh, I went out into the garden, you know, and as I bent down to pull up some carrots, I lost track of time. But where? In the garden, in the ground. I got lost on the path up to Tendrier because of the ultrasound. You know, the ultrasound from the wind turbines. Ukalo, the turbines don't make ultrasonic waves, and anyway, only animals and children can hear them. That's it, I got lost because I was looking for somewhere I could hear them, looking for the time, the time when I was young. I was wondering where the hearing I had when I was twenty could have got to. When he's like that, full of forgetfulness and ideas, a wink and a smile at the ready, we find ourselves wishing the gaps in his memory were even wider, so we could listen to him fill them with captivating stories. But not in winter, never then. Sometimes in winter I suddenly realize he's gone out in the middle of the night and I run after him, not even putting my jacket on. I find him out there in the moonlight, sitting in the snow lit up bright as day, and I shout, When are you going to get on with it and die? I scream like a crazy woman, my head pounding from the cold and from running around in my nightie.

I don't want him to die, because I'm very fond of him, more than just fond. But a life like that, well, I'm not sure it really is a life, and that's partly our fault also. I feel ashamed, even though I keep telling myself it's better than a home or the mental hospital, and my husband and I are sick of social services breathing down our necks, so we're just waiting for it to be over, all the while making money from the tourists he attracts.

My husband says it's no way to treat someone, and that we're going to end up in trouble with the Farmers' Mutual because we can't declare our automatic tour guide. His papers went out of date decades ago. We do wonder what the police are waiting for, with everything you see on the news about families being sent back, but not him, oh no. They know him and they know full well what the situation is, and yet they've never come knocking. We're not above board and that bothers my husband. We often argue about Ukalo, like we used to argue about the children, but worse because we haven't got the patience we had when we were young.

The social services lady comes to check on him every so often and I see her glancing around to check that the place is clean and Ukalo is decently dressed. At the slightest sign of neglect it'll be off to the home with him. I wonder how they'd manage it, given that he's not even legal. But I'm not worried about that. The house is neat and Ukalo looks well turned out. He's always been very meticulous.

His house is tiny, just one room on the ground floor and a bedroom with a little washroom upstairs.

It's connected to our *gîte* by this shelter where he does his automatic guiding. The shelter's open to the elements and our grandchildren tried to give Ukalo the nickname 'bats in the belfry', because the wind whistles all around him and because he's going batty. But the name never stuck; Ukalo's the automatic guide, not the village idiot.

My husband and I live on the other side of the *gîte* and our top floor overlooks the shelter. That's all there is of our little hamlet, these few buildings.

All the buildings belonged to our grandparents and our grandfather's brother, my great-uncle, who was a bachelor his whole life and was always just known as 'Uncle'. It was Uncle who brought Ukalo here in the 1950s. I was very little and my sister had just been born. Uncle was over forty and he must surely have known that having a foreigner on the farm wouldn't attract a woman there, quite the reverse. His older brother, our grandfather, had about ten children and lots of grandchildren already, so that would be enough. A woman was more expensive than a foreigner, and a foreigner would be a better worker than a woman.

We had a shortage of farm labourers. The Polish had a shortage of everything. Uncle lived in Ukalo's house. Or, well, the other way around, the opposite really, but anyway. Ukalo came to live in Uncle's house, in his bedroom. They had two single beds and were almost the same age. Ukalo and Uncle lived their bachelor lives together like two roommates, communicating in Uncle's language, a patois that I could never understand, a sort of Occitan peppered with family words, invented by the family and for the family, a blood language that wasn't passed down beyond Father's generation and that only Ukalo still speaks today. He hasn't got anyone to speak it to, so he doesn't use it much, just a few words here and there in automatic mode for the fascinated tourists. He and Uncle shared their little world of words and habits until Uncle died about ten years ago. The old man left his house to the labourer, his friend, his foreign brother, his Ukalo, as he used to call him.

My parents had already taken over the farm after my grandparents died, Father being the only one of their ten kids to accept the slavery of the fields.

It wasn't long before it drove him to suicide, after he'd let my little sister be scattered all over the pumpkin field. Mother waited until I was eighteen, seeing as I was the only one left after my sister died, before finally giving in to cancer. We divided everything up and I was the only one who wanted to stay with Uncle and Ukalo, me with my scatterbrain, my husband and my three children. My husband worked nearby, so it was convenient really.

When Uncle died, our three children had already gone off to their new lives, city girls and proud of it. We'd just started renting out the *gîte* to give ourselves something to do. By then my husband was retired from the postal service and I had no more children to look after, or even any animals, just the housework in the *gîte* every Saturday, so my brothers and sisters didn't give it a second thought. I was the one who'd look after Uncle's heir.

The whole family was there on the morning of Uncle's funeral, my brothers, sisters, aunts, uncles and cousins, but they were all gone again by the evening. We couldn't have put them all up here in any case. Ukalo came to our house for a coffee. He watched them getting ready to go, muttering in his language or perhaps in Uncle's language, like he always does when he wants to say something without saying anything, when he wants to be heard without being understood – or the opposite, I'm not sure. He put the cup down on the tablecloth, taking an age to open his big hands, as though it were impossible to let go of the coffee cup. Then, very quickly, decisively, he got up without saying a word, not even in his or in Uncle's language. He left and went over to Uncle's house, or his house as it was now. He stopped to say hello to the guests who'd just arrived at the *gîte*. They were the brazen sort and, while there was nobody around because we were all at the funeral, they'd managed to open the *gîte*'s back door, which gives on to the shelter in front of Uncle's house. Ukalo stood there surprised and silent as they replied to his hello and started telling him how much they liked our part of the world, the plateau, being on holiday, and then all about their lives, and blah blah blah. Ukalo sat down on the little bench in the shelter and he started talking too, about everything and nothing, about the fox that a little girl had killed with her bare hands in January, our latest little news story, then about Uncle, my little sister and people from the village who were dead now. There was no stopping him, and there were certainly plenty of dead people to talk about, more than there were living ones. Ukalo talked as if he were reading aloud, with an expressionless, rhythmical delivery, already in automatic mode, and those rude tourists closed the door, saying, Right, we're off for our dinner, bye, thank you, but still it wasn't a very polite thing to do, if you ask me.

Ever since that evening, since Uncle's funeral, Ukalo has been the automatic tour guide. At first we tried our best to make him stop. We didn't want him bothering people. But Ukalo would spit on the ground with rage every time I tried to intervene. We ended up letting him get on with it.

Whoever's staying in the *gîte* has only to open the back door any time between eight in the morning and midday, and then again from one to five, and Ukalo will begin his stories, not letting anyone reply or comment. You open the door and he talks, and to make him stop, you have to close the door.

He does the guiding every day except Sunday, because he's a Christian, but mainly because he doesn't want to miss 'The Sunday Phone Call' on Christian Radio France. Sometimes he'll skip Mass without complaining if I can't be bothered to drive him down to the village and wait for him in a bar with a book, because, personally, if I've got to sit through a load of old twaddle I'd rather it was in a book than in church. But I haven't always got a book on the go, so one day we agreed that we'd go to Mass about once a month, that was plenty, and he didn't grumble, not in his language or Uncle's, or even ours. But as for missing 'The Sunday Phone Call', no chance. He can't do without it. It's a kind of obsession, or a kind of food, like air and water, a bit of time all to himself. It's a programme where people call in and leave a message for family members in prison, via the radio. Ukalo is addicted to it. He moves right up close to the radio with his mouth open, listening greedily. He sits there hoovering up all the messages so eagerly, inhaling them through his mouth, that I sometimes wonder if he's done time in prison back home, or if he feels as though he's in prison here, in his shelter. It's as though he's expecting a message from someone, maybe from his family in Poland, or from Uncle, speaking from beyond the grave via CRF, like a good stupid Christian. If he thinks he's going to find them all in heaven, Uncle, Father, Mother and my little sister, then he's just as thick as the holidaymakers who stand listening by the back door, thinking that what he's saying is genuine local folklore. As if.

Often the tales he tells aren't authentic legends, and it isn't just that they're made up, they're not even from around here. They're Ukalo's stories, things that he's found in old newspapers, not quite a hundred years old but not far off. He weaves them all together and adds bits of his own memories from Poland, spices them up with some family patois and sticks in a few local place names to make them sound bona fide. I caught him at it one evening. He was reading his tatty newspapers, completely absorbed, looking for who knows what on dog-eared old maps, and looking inside himself too, I think. He had a glazed expression, as though he was peering into the cracks in his memory. He looked drunk, sitting there at the table with his head in his big, shaky hands and papers scattered around him on the tablecloth in a huge mess. He was embarrassed and tried to convince me that he'd got the newspapers out to peel some vegetables, but he hadn't picked any vegetables that day and yesterday's soup was already heating up on the wood stove. He couldn't fool me. It was the papers themselves, and his whole life along with them, that he was peeling to replenish his stock of stories.

My little sister's death doesn't need inventing, and when he tells it to the people staying in the *gîte* he doesn't embellish it with local colour. He delivers it straight, raw, hardly like a story at all.

For a few months now, in spite of all the coffees, medicines and glasses of water that I make him drink, he's been getting more and more dehydrated. The inside of his mouth hurts because he hasn't got enough saliva. When he wants to speak, he constantly has to open and close his mouth, and his lips make a series of rapid, regular sounds, slightly moist clicks like a suckling baby.

It was to the accompaniment of these delicate lapping sounds that I heard him recite the story of my sister's death yet again, just over a month ago, as I was closing the shutters on the early December darkness. It was nearly five o'clock. He was telling it to the latest person to open the door, a boy come to have a fag in the bitter cold. No doubt it was a good excuse to give his parents: popping out for a quick smoke before the automatic guide knocked off for the day. He was shivering hard, caught unawares by the sudden, savage nightfall that we have in these parts, when the air shines with a cold that catches you by the throat and when you feel as though each breath is tearing at your insides. I don't know if the cigarette made this feeling worse or better but, with touchingly awkward embarrassment, he asked if he could move closer to him, to the guide, and to the fire. Ukalo carried on with his story, told to the rhythm of the baby-like suckling sounds, without replying, in his usual mad, obsessive way. The boy sat down next to him, the cigarette a red spot in the blue of the snow streaked with ash plumes. I'd just closed the shutters on the top floor and didn't want to hear any more. I knew what happened next. I heard it despite myself, as if Ukalo's voice, so thin and age-worn, as if this voice deformed by the sucking of words seeking water, as if this diminished voice, reduced to incessant blinks of sound, as if this parched voice could travel so far and penetrate the shutters and double glazing of the window where I rested my forehead.

I know what happened next. Father left the tractor in the pumpkin field just behind the house without bothering to take off the rotary tiller, annoyed at being interrupted in the middle of preparing the seed beds, and ran towards the house to answer the telephone. Mother had come out to the doorstep, my sister and me clinging to her skirt, and was waving her arms to tell him to come and take the call. He came in with his boots still on, cursing Mother. She followed him once she had detached us from her legs. My sister ran off towards the tractor but I didn't, I knew we weren't allowed, and I told her not to but she didn't listen, that little two-year-old silly. Father came out again almost straight away, still cross, went back to the field and got on the tractor. He started it up again, and when he heard me screaming louder and higher than the sound of the engine, when he felt the tiller jam, he was really beside himself, absolutely furious this time. He stopped the engine, he jumped out of the cabin like a madman, telling me to shut it. He went round and bent down to disengage the tiller. He stood up again immediately. He came back to the house and I was running behind him, I overtook him. Mother was on the doorstep again, immobile and grey, rooted to the spot, as though she were made of cement and stupefaction. I grabbed on to her. Father shoved past us and went straight to the cupboard for his rifle. I remember I ran to Uncle's house and straight into Ukalo's arms when Mother collapsed.

The tourists at the *gîte* came to say goodbye and thank you. They went off in a sparkle of frost and a gleam of bodywork, and there was so much glitter in their going that it brought tears to my eyes. They hadn't once opened the back door.

It's past midday and Ukalo is still sitting in the shelter. He must have lost track of time. I go to him and bend down to give him the Tupperware. He hasn't invented some convoluted, fantastical reason for forgetting what time it is. He gets up with a new heaviness, and without looking at me he goes back inside.

I'm cold. I go home when I hear the lonely bing of the microwave.

Silent B

Lauren Elkin

Debt is one of those English words you'd never know how to pronounce if you weren't a native speaker. The b is silent. Like in thumb. But it's there, it sticks out, like a sore thumb. That b next to that t. How often does that happen? If you're British, you're used to seeing the B and the T together, as in British Telecom, as in BT Tower. There are groupings we get used to. Groupings that become natural, until the day we look at them askance, and ask: really? And the doubted answer—an-swerve —is yes, really.

According to the Free Dictionary on the internet, the silent B came about because of the particular combination of Latin, Old English, and/or Old French that provided its source. "Sometimes," we learn, "as in the word *doubt*, the silent B was added to the word to help it *resemble* Latin or draw a clearer connection to a related Latin term (in this case, *dubitare*, from which *dubious* is derived)."

That description makes it sound like one fine day along came a Redactor who decided to make sense out of these pesky originary words and clear things up once and for all. *J'ai un doute là.* This word should sound more like Latin! Let's add a silent B to it and make it doubt.

These oddities create resonances across the words themselves, drawing them into a dubious family: Doubt. Debt. Subtle. The B meets T in subterfuge but no longer remains silent.

We have to scrutinize the things that appear natural and just as quickly unnatural. Is this system working for us? Could it work better? Has it undergone certain monstrously delightful modifications, and is it time to retrace how that came to happen? The dubious nature of debt is as naturalized as that silent B. Debt in the wrong hands becomes a tool of power, when it ought to be a tool of community. We are all in debt to one another. There is no redactor at the source of it all, no original lender. We live in a web of exchanges; the debt is never paid. Only forgiven. The sooner we can get this through our numbskulls, the better off we'll be.

The Return of the Argonauts
Clemens Meyer, *translated by* Katy Derbyshire

They came from a realm of shadows that had formed over decades in the rear yards of the Coal Quarter, small factories with round, soot-blackened chimneys where pigeons perched when no smoke rose from the outlets, workshops, coal merchants, dilapidated buildings with small birch forests growing on their roofs, empty, decaying factories, passageways to the road and to the light, but the light outside was murky too; shadows lay over these yards where I'd met them many years ago, and as I returned to them now the sun was shining, and nothing fitted together any more.

I had got off the train at the main station and put my bag in a luggage locker, even though I was planning to go to my mother's place in the evening, she had made up my old bed—'I've built your bed for you,'—I had called her from the train but now I switched off the phone, put the slip of paper with the numbers in the inside pocket of my coat and went to the East Side, to the big station's eastern side exit.

You don't get a key these days, you don't have to pull a key out of the metal door these days, you just get a little slip of paper that pops out of a slot, a wall full of safes holding travel bags.

The concourse was filled with the clack-clack-clack of wheeled cases, the weekend travellers wheeling and rushing to their trains at my back...

Had they ever left the Coal Quarter? Now and then, they'd visited their half-brother, who they called their eighth-brother because he looked nothing like them, and who lived somewhere near Cologne. I'd seen him a few times when he visited his eighth-brothers and his mother in the Coal Quarter, a short, thin, bespectacled man whose head always seemed to bob to and fro on his thin neck. I remembered that H. had worked for his eighth-brother for a couple of months, he was running a furniture transport place in Cologne at the time and H. had often done removals here in our own town, he was a good removals man who knew all the tricks, used straps and belts, worked from his legs to protect his back, and knew how to stow cupboard after cupboard, more and more furniture mysteriously fitting into the far too small back of the truck; most people think all you need is muscle power.

They did have muscle power, H. and his little brother K., a bit less than two years younger, who was a bricklayer, or was training as a bricklayer when I met them.

Back then, we thought H. would stay in the big city in the West, but then he was back after a couple of months. 'Why should I stay in Cologne?' he'd said. 'I might as well shift furniture here.'

Had they ever left the Coal Quarter?

I'd met H. at the station one time, years before. I was reminded of it when I was standing by the little metal door earlier, the door with my bag behind it, and running my hand over the lock mechanism, but all that happened was a piece of paper popping out of a gap, a slip with a number code on it.

I couldn't remember where I'd been coming from or where I was going, or whether I'd just been strolling around the station as I do so often, watching the travellers. H. was wearing his uniform and his army backpack, he was on the way to catch a train to the barracks. I can't remember where he was stationed; it was only for a year. They'd exempted me for health reasons.

'Oi, mate!' he called when he saw me, and then he laughed so loudly that his laugh and his voice echoed beneath the arches across the platforms, pigeons flapped upwards, 'Oiiii-aaate,' and not much later we were in the pub next to the staircase that led down from the platforms into the ticket hall, drinking beer and a few shots of brown spirits until his train had departed without him.

Then we got in his car, which he'd parked in a side street, a tiny old dented Renault 5 with no MOT, full of those hanging air-freshener trees, and drove through the night without a destination, from here to there, the windows wound down, 'Let's go and see M., let's go home,' and when we'd almost got to M.'s place—he lived in the Coal Quarter too—we had to go back again because H. had left his army backpack in the pub and it had all his stuff and his papers in it. The backpack was gone but we found it in the end under a bench on one of the many platforms. It was empty but H. just laughed, 'Let's go and see M., the sky's so clear tonight.'

My old schoolfriend M., who had introduced me to the brothers, M. the friend of the stars with the big telescope on a tripod up on the roof next to a puny birch tree, M. who had led me into the realm of shadows, those rear yards of the Coal Quarter where strange people dwelled, like figures from legend, fairy-tale dwarfs, giants, accursed women, led me to the realm of shadows and nightmares... but when we were there, when we drank with them, we became part of those dark tales ourselves...

We sat at M.'s place and drank, and then we went up on the roof to his telescope and looked at the stars. M. knew all the constellations. We ran across the yard to wake K., who was asleep already because he had to get to the building site in the morning, but he just turned around in his bed, 'Leave me alone, you're insane,' and so we went on drinking without him, M., H. and me.

Castor and Pollux. The inseparable brothers who once set out with the Argonauts. In the constellation of Gemini. One mortal, the other immortal, that was how M. explained it back then, slurring his words. 'Who are the Argonauts?' H. asked.

'Crazy guys looking for something, thousands of years ago.' M. held onto his telescope tripod, pressed his eye so hard to the eyepiece I was scared it would push back into its socket, and that was how he looked out into space, at the constellations, at Castor and Pollux. Did he tell us all the stories of the Argonauts that night?

In the morning, the M.P.s came to pick up H. Everyone in the Coal Quarter hated the military police. They were police, after all. When they led H., still half-cut, across the rear yard, all the old grannies leaned out of their windows and yelled at the two M.P.s in their pale grey uniforms with the guns on their belts, and one old lady tipped her potato peelings out over them, no, more in front of them, and they trod on the potato peelings with H., and I trod on them later too, a rag-rug of potato peel. I ran to the yard's entrance, to the road, but the M.P.s and H. were gone.

I blinked at the midday sun and left the station behind me and walked very slowly along the narrow streets to the East, to the Coal Quarter.

I sat down in Inge's Corner, where we often used to go. I wanted a drink before I rang on K.'s doorbell. He was back at his mother's place now.

Inge's Corner had got smaller, shrunk down.

At first I thought it was just my memories misleading me, an endless bar full of people drinking, their voices making the room even bigger, a dome of voices and sounds, the room getting larger and larger, mists wafting above the tables, flushed faces moving in the mist as though distorted through optical lenses, rolled-up shirtsleeves revealing strange tattoos, glasses of all sizes on the tables, playing-cards floating through the air as if in slow motion, a fug of beer and sweat and grease, Inge used to cook herself back then and there was hot food round the clock, a smell that mixed with the fog of the cigarettes, and outside the chimneys puffed out smoke. The coal merchants did good business until the old buildings got done up or torn down and the coal stoves gradually disappeared, the coal merchants gradually disappeared, the Coal Quarter gradually disappeared.

Inge's Corner had shrunk down, a new wall put up through the middle of the taproom, and the big kitchen Inge used to bring trays of food from was gone too. I could tell by a sign behind the bar that they only served sausages with buns. And only a few people were sitting at the few remaining tables, the smoke of an occasional cigarette dispersing thinly into the room... What was behind the wall? A storage space, a flat? A shop? I got up and went outside to look at the building properly and solve the puzzle of the shrunken space, and as I turned back to the bar just before the door I saw a soldier sitting there, must have been there all along. In uniform, his beret rolled up next to his beer, next to a shot of brown spirits. He looked at me briefly, I nodded at him, and he raised his shot glass and drank.

It was cool outside, the sun setting behind the buildings. The Inge's Corner sign wasn't lit up yet, and it didn't light up later, once it got dark. I looked up the wall of the building. They'd done up the whole street, years before. But the plaster was beginning to go grey again, peeling in places, already weathered, damp creeping out of the ground into the brickwork—weren't there even a few little birch trees growing on the roof?—I tipped my head back further, clear blue summer sky, the house went on slowly going grey, weathering as though it felt uncomfortable under all the new plaster, the houses had all been grey and almost black in the Coal Quarter, and they were going grey again now, even though the coal merchants had disappeared.

The brothers H. and K.—their father had been a coal merchant, they were rich and influential, the coal merchants, back when thousands and thousands of coal stoves puffed smoke into the sky... When he died he coughed as if he wanted to expel all the dust of those years, coal dust, mountains of coal dust that they'd put in the sacks and weighed along with the coal, dust that mixed in with the smoke of the chimneys, the factories, the cigarettes, dust that he coughed up when he died, H. trying to bring him back, H.'s hands on his chest.

'Where were you then?' his little brother would ask me later, the hour of the

Argonauts, 'where the hell were you back then?'

Standing outside the building, standing in front of Inge's Corner, my head still tipped back so far it was hurting my neck, I saw the scaffolding in front of the façades, the scaffolding growing up to the sky, winding around the buildings, the birch forests on the roofs getting chopped down, we're standing on the scaffolding planks, H. and me, we work on building sites when we need the money and when H. doesn't pick up any removals, his little brother the bricklayer gets us jobs, we're builder's mates, labourers, shaft workers, gutters, the demolition brigade... We cough dust, red brick dust sticks to our tissues like nosebleeds, we wear mouth guards like doctors in surgery, we call the protectors 'Laddie' and the huge hammers we use to tear down fireplaces and whole walls, we call 'Rover', we lug cement sacks and plasterboard up stairs and down stairs, we grip pneumatic hammers, our bodies vibrate, we yell into the noise, the old grey plaster leaps off the bricks, the façades, the walls of the buildings, thunders down the inside of the scaffolding onto the road, onto the pavement, dust rises, we stand on the roofs of the Coal Quarter wearing yellow helmets, they too are coated in dust, we see M.'s telescope, still on its tripod next to the puny birch tree, they haven't got that far yet even though M.'s gone now... No, he was standing up there as H. and I worked on the roofs, the roofs of the Coal Quarter and the roofs of the town, he waved and looked at us through his telescope, the times are mingling together, it's grown cold, no light in Inge's Corner—when did M. disappear?—when did H. disappear?—when did I disappear?—death was on the prowl in our buildings, in our yards.

'Will you get me a drink in?' the soldier asked. He was no longer there when I opened the door to Inge's Corner again—had I been away so long, outside so long?—but then I saw the rolled-up beret next to an empty shot glass.

'Will you get me a drink in?' he asked again as he stepped out of the little gap in the wall that led to the toilets, despite the loss of space, and I said, 'What'll you have, mate?' I looked at him; he was at least ten years younger than me, hard to say exactly, but his eyes looked old and tired.

'The same as you're drinking.'

I looked at the bottles on the shelves behind the bar, just a few sorts of spirits and liqueurs, like in the old days, clear schnapps, brown schnapps, Castor and Pollux, H. used to prefer brown spirits to clear, he laughs and raises his glass to me, an endless chain of small glasses full of that brown schnapps moving around his head, glinting dully in the pub dusk... The landlord was somewhere in the bar room with the few drinkers, Inge had disappeared years before, sold the place while I was still living in our town.

I turned around and called out into the room, 'Two beers, two browns.' 'Coming,' the landlord called from somewhere. The soldier pressed his beret together with both hands while the landlord got our drinks.

I looked at the soldier but he seemed to be looking through the walls... H. had almost always been behind bars during his national service, had looked through the walls there because he'd punched his sergeant with his removal-man coal-merchant fist and because he often missed the train after the weekends.

'Two beers, two jokers.' The landlord put our drinks down on the bar. The soldier pulled the glasses over and raised the shot glass, and I waited for him to say something, to drink to something, but we drank in silence. No toasts.

'Where did you do service?' the soldier asks, putting his empty shot glass down slowly.

'I didn't do service,' I said. 'Flat feet.'

He nodded. 'Probably better that way. Will you get me another?'

'Did your pay come late?'

'No.' Now he looked at me and I knew that look, knew it from the pubs and bars in the Coal Quarter just before insanity broke loose, H.'s little brother K. often used to have that look, his pupils got smaller and smaller and then bigger again, like his eyes were breathing in and out. 'Alright, soldier, why not?', a white glow, and behind that glow waited insanity, waited war, waited the first blow, K. slammed his glass into some guy's face, some guy or other who'd been annoying him for minutes, blood ran down skin, someone hit out at K., his brother turned up and punched some face or other, glass smashed, someone yelled, someone laughed, I stayed put on my seat and there was a strange calm in me, I sensed the way it all felt inevitable, the ticking-over of ancient rituals, old and older than the Coal Quarter, it was a realm of shadows, the walls dissolved and I could see into the flats, saw the old grannies sitting silently at their tables, saw the drinkers lying trembling in their beds, saw M. leaning over a book, the ancient myths and the stars—when had he disappeared, and why had he disappeared?—and I saw H., dancing with his girlfriend all alone between the tables and chairs, their bodies touching, his head on her shoulder, some old nineties hit playing, was it here in Inge's Corner or in one of the other Coal Quarter pubs?

And the soldier drank again. 'Was pretty dusty *out there*, eh?' I said, and he nodded.

'Still is,' putting the shot glass slowly down next to the empty one from our first round. The landlord went to clear it away, reaching for it, but the soldier said, 'Leave it, it looks nice like that.'

And the soldier drank again, three small empty glasses in front of him, three small empty glasses in front of me. I turned for a moment and called out 'I'll pay now, then.' The landlord was back at one of the tables, drinking with one of the few punters. His shot glass shone green, peppermint, that was what the old drinkers drank when their stomachs couldn't take any more hard spirits.

'I guess you're not from round here, mate,' said the soldier. 'I've never seen you in…' He halted and ran his forefinger through the air, drew a semi-circle around his face, drawing the Coal Quarter into space like a one-handed conductor.

'I've been away a long time,' I said, 'I used to spend a lot of time here, in the old days, had good friends round here.' I touched the three empty glasses, which I'd pushed close together.

The soldier nodded. He took a squashed cigarette pack out of the inside pocket of his khaki jacket, pulled out a crooked cigarette, which he carefully stroked into shape and tapped on the bar a couple of times before he put it between his lips, then he put the box down next to his rolled-up beret. He was looking at the wall behind the bar again, seemed not to be paying me any more attention. But once I'd paid and gone to the door, he said—and his voice sounded strangely dull because he didn't turn around to the door but spoke to the wall instead, his words bouncing off it through the smaller room of Inge's Corner—'Come back soon, mate, I'm always here.'

I woke with a start. It was dark and cold. I was sitting in the little park opposite M.'s house, actually just a patch of grass with a kids' playground. I looked at my watch. Only six. I had dreamed of the soldier. He didn't take a squashed cigarette pack out of his uniform pocket, it was a stable one, firm, and in my dream, it seemed beautiful, white, a white glow with a red triangle, what a gorgeous red, I wanted to touch it, the white and red, in my dream. The death warning was printed on the box in some foreign language, so I couldn't read it. And the soldier said, 'They make our poisons pretty beautiful, don't they?' It wasn't until my dream that I saw he was wearing a medal on his uniform jacket.

The windows in M.'s building were dark, probably no one lived there now. It hadn't been done up and they'd torn down a few buildings a bit further along the road, I could see the empty lots in the darkness and a bit behind them the big road leading out of town, lights moving there, red and yellow, that was the world of fast lights, the world of streams and networks. Was the telescope still up on the roof on its tripod? M. the friend of the stars, who knew all the constellations and told us stories when we sat with him on that roof. Castor and Pollux and the Argonauts. 'Go away,' he said to me, 'try something new somewhere. You're one of the clever boys.'

'Hey, hey,' I said, 'we're the same age! And what about *you*?'

He smiled and adjusted his glasses. 'Me? I'm doing fine right here.'

The bench I was sitting on felt damp and cold. I got up. K.'s mother lived a few doors down. I stopped by M.'s front door. The names on the bells were barely legible now. I put the palm of my hand on the bells, wanted to press them all but then I didn't, just stood there, stood for a while in the dark entrance to the yard, one foot on the stone threshold, my palm on the bell buttons.

She opened the door. She didn't recognize me straight away, and then she hugged me. She almost fell as she did, letting go of a walking stick. 'Come in.'

I bent down, picked up the stick and handed it to her. She limped through the flat ahead of me.

'K.'s not here,' she said once we'd sat down in the living room, her on the big couch, me on one of the armchairs. The ashtray on the coffee table was full of butts, one still smoking. An open can of beer and a half-full glass next to the ashtray.

'Beers in the fridge if you want one.'

'Yes, thanks.' I got up again. I'd almost forgotten, after all the years, that I was a friend of the family. On the way to the kitchen I passed the wall unit. In the cabinet, between glasses and china figurines, was a glittery black briquette with a gold-framed photo on top of it. She and her husband. The coal merchant, the coal deliveryman, the king of coal, the king of the Coal Quarter, the father of Castor and Pollux. He had his arms around his wife, who was now coughing behind me. On either side of the briquette were photos of her sons. Behind the briquette, a photo of a field of graves leant against the back of the cabinet. It must be somewhere outside of town. I went down the hall to the kitchen.

The door to K.'s room was there, the room the brothers had shared until they moved out and then back in and then out again. Where was K.?

I was scared of what his mother would tell me. I squatted down for a while in the light of the open fridge, then I took out a beer and went back to the living room.

'He always said you'd come back one day.' She'd leant her crutch up against the sofa, smoking and taking sips from her glass.

I wanted to ask if she meant H. or his brother. But I just opened the can of beer, a bit of foam spilling onto my hand.

'He's in hospital,' she said. And again, I didn't know exactly which brother she meant. H.'s time in hospital was long gone, but she lived in a realm of shadows.

'What's... what's the matter with K.?' I asked. And again, I was afraid of what she'd say, their mother. Had H. come to fetch his brother? Castor and Pollux, the inseparable brothers, like old women sometimes did with their old husbands, or the other way around...

I tried to remember... What had I felt when I heard first about H.'s, then about M.'s disappearance? I didn't come to town, not then.

It was an old world slowly disappearing, and its inhabitants disappeared with it. The Coal Quarter with all its odd people, like figures from legends and fairy-tales… Famous drinkers who got thinner and frailer like that Phineus M. told us about, an old man wasting away on an island, punished by the gods, and in the end all they could drink was peppermint liqueur and they'd do terrible things to each other on the drink, coal merchants who couldn't sell coal because the stoves were no longer burning, faded tattoos on old skin, old grannies with elbows on faded cushions, looking out of the window all day long, kids who lived in the pubs like their fathers and sat in the rear yards by night, sat on the kerb and drank, moved out and back in again, death was on the prowl in our yards, in our buildings.

'What's the matter with K.?' I asked again, because she hadn't answered; perhaps hadn't heard me. Or she had answered and I hadn't heard *her*. She had taken some tobacco out of a big tin and crumbled it into a kind of cigarette-rolling machine.

'It's... not his body,' she said and she lit the finished cigarette. 'It's his mind. He doesn't understand things any more.'

'Things,' I said.

'Why you never came. Why he's all alone, why his brother's gone, and M., you remember M., don't you?'

'Of course,' I said.

'Of course,' she said and reached for her cigarette from the edge of the ashtray.

We were sitting on the roof, only the tripod left without the telescope next to the half-parched birch tree.

'I come and go,' said K.

He was sitting next to me, his legs dangling in the darkness where the roof dropped off steeply to the rear yard.

'Oh, no, not that,' said K., and I could almost feel him dangling his legs, moving his feet up and down like a kid, 'not that. That wouldn't be OK.'

'No,' I said, 'it wouldn't.'

'He just went yellow,' K. said, 'just like that. I took him to hospital... He couldn't...'

'And you?' I asked.

'...couldn't walk any more. Down there...' he pointed down into the darkness of the yard. The light of a half-moon, somewhere above us, behind us, only sparsely illuminated the roof, and the clouds covered it and migrated, and the shadows moved, and nothing fitted together any more; his father, his brother, M.

The building's front door I'd stood outside just earlier, my hand on the doorbells of those long-uninhabited spaces—K. had kicked it in, he'd been there suddenly when I walked across the rear yard of his mother's building to the passageway, he'd been standing in the passageway to the road, right by the wall so I couldn't see him at all to begin with.

'Oi, mate,' he'd whispered, and in the close, dark passageway his hoarse whisper had echoed strangely, 'Oiiii-aaate.'

'I come and I go.' It was only now I felt my hand was still on K.'s shoulder. It moved as he spoke.

'What do I want in those white rooms?'

'Don't they treat you well?'

He laughed quietly. 'Everyone treats me well.'

'I'm sorry,' I said, and I took my hand off his shoulder.

'Don't be, what for? I always knew you'd come. He can't walk any more, we have to get him out of here.' He moved his legs, properly swinging them, his feet briefly coming into view in the light of the half-moon.

'And M.?' I asked.

'Our good friend M.' Suddenly he was all there again, perfectly compos mentis, and he turned and looked at me, his eyes looking old and tired, no clouds across the half-moon.

He had kicked in the door downstairs and it seemed to me, as he slammed his foot against the dark wood of the door, as though it would open before the wood splintered, before his foot kicked the door off its hinges. Castor and Pollux and the Argonauts.

'Once H. was gone, all M. did was sit up here. All we did was sit up here.'

'And he...'

'Once you were gone, all we did was sit up here. No, that's not true. You did come and you gave that nice speech. Over there, outside of town.'

'Yes,' I said, 'I did.'

'Yes, you did.' He leaned back, let his upper body fall back onto the damp roofing, a few moss-covered tiles still dotted here and there. I hadn't been in town, back then. I'd heard about their disappearances but I didn't want to come back to the Coal Quarter, I just couldn't do it, and I'd only seen their disappearances in my dreams.

'He went yellow. Overnight. Just like that. Stomach, liver, gall bladder, who knows?'

'And then he...?'

'They said only old men got it. It was like a miracle that he had it. He was too young, you get it, too young to go yellow just like that.'

I leaned back, lay down next to him so I didn't fall off the roof into the dark of the rear yards. I looked out across the roofs. Somewhere out there was the station where I'd just arrived, and around the station and so far away was the flicker of the town, which seemed to be a different town, and the tenements in the Coal Quarter were dark satellites.

'What did he call him, that skinny old man? Phineus?'

'You mean M.?' I asked.

'Yeah.'

'Yeah, those were his stories,' I said.

'Can you tell what anything is up there?'

We looked at the stars. 'No,' I said. 'Maybe the Plough.'

'There was this woman once, well, I wouldn't say a woman...'

And then he told a story about a toolbox on Phineus's island, and M., there for some reason, confused and alone, and Phineus and his friends and the woman and the toolbox full of tools, but I didn't want to hear it, the dark bad fables of the Coal Quarter.

'In and out,' said K., 'in and out.'

'What can you do?' I said.

'Drink peppermint,' said K., 'fall down.'

Then we stopped talking and lay on the roof and watched the half-moon setting.

After a while I went to my mother's. 'I've built you your bed.' My bag was still behind the metal wall of safes but I couldn't fetch it, didn't want to fetch it either that night. The slip of paper with the numbers on it was probably by the birch tree, by the tripod, where I'd sat with them one last time, the return of the Argonauts M. had always told us about. And they really were up there with us, on the roof.

K. had dug up both caskets full of ashes and put them in one of the chimneys, up on the roof; he hadn't told me when: months ago, years ago, days ago. I'd looked at him and I knew straight away they were really in there, knew he'd 'brought them home,' as he called it.

They came from a realm of shadows that had formed over decades in the rear yards of the Coal Quarter, small factories with round, soot-blackened chimneys where pigeons perched when no smoke was rising from them, workshops, coal merchants, dilapidated buildings with small birch forests growing on their roofs, empty, decaying factories, passageways to the road and to the light, but the light outside was only murky too; shadows lay over these yards where I'd met them many years ago, and as I returned to them now I realized it had all disappeared long ago and yet would always be there.

Notes on Contributors

Wayne Koestenbaum has published nineteen books of poetry, criticism, and fiction, including *Notes on Glaze, The Pink Trance Notebooks, My 1980s & Other Essays, Hotel Theory, Best-Selling Jewish Porn Films, Andy Warhol, Humiliation, Jackie Under My Skin,* and *The Queen's Throat* (a National Book Critics Circle Award finalist). His newest book of poetry, *Camp Marmalade,* was published this spring. He has exhibited his paintings in solo shows at White Columns (New York), 356 Mission (Los Angeles), and the University of Kentucky Art Museum. His first piano/vocal record, *Lounge Act,* was released by Ugly Duckling Presse Records in 2017; he has given musical performances at The Kitchen, REDCAT, Centre Pompidou, The Walker Art Center, and the Renaissance Society. He is a Distinguished Professor of English, Comparative Literature, and French at the CUNY Graduate Center in New York City.

Glykeria Patramani is a writer based in Athens, Greece working within the fields of cinema and documentary.

Imogen Cassels's poems have appeared in the *London Review of Books*, *Blackbox Manifold*, *Cumulus*, *Datableed*, *Ambit*, and on the London Underground.

Will Oldham makes songs under the *nom de guerre* Bonnie 'Prince' Billy. Most of his lyrics have been collected recently in book form under the title *Songs of Love and Horror*. Bonnie 'Prince' Billy's most recent record is *I Made a Place*. He lives in Louisville, KY with his wife and daughter.

Diego Fonseca is the editor and author of numerous books of narrative journalism including *Crecer a golpes* (Penguin USA), *Sam no es mi tío* (Alfaguara), and *Tiembla* (Almadía). His fiction includes the novel *La vigilia* and the short story collections *El azar y los héroes*, *El último comunista de Miami* and *South Beach*. He teaches journalism at the Gabriel García Márquez Foundation and is a columnist for the *New York Times* in Spanish.

Ellen Jones is a researcher, editor, and translator from Spanish. She writes about multilingualism and contemporary Latin American literature, including for publications like *The Guardian*, *The Times Literary Supplement* and *The Irish Times*. Her translation of Rodrigo Fuentes's short story collection *Trout, Belly Up* is published by Charco Press (2019) and her translation of Bruno Lloret's novel *Nancy* was published by Giramondo (2020).

Hao Guang Tse [謝皓光] is a Singaporean poet and editor, assembled with parts from Hong Kong and Malaysia. His first full-length poetry collection, *Deeds of Light,* was shortlisted for the 2016 Singapore Literature Prize. He is a 2016 fellow of the University of Iowa's International Writing Program, and the 2018 National Writer-in-Residence at Nanyang Technological University. He has things in *Asian American Writers' Workshop, Sand Journal, AJAR, High Chair, Entropy, Third Coast* and *Prairie Schooner*. A new work-in-progress is tentatively titled *I Get Buzzed Seeing Your Hand's Just Left.*

Geoffrey Mak is a writer who divides his time between New York and Berlin. His writing has appeared in *Artforum, Art in America, Mask, Guernica*, and *The Los Angeles Review of Books.*

Astrid Alben is a poet and translator. Her next collection, *Plainspeak*, was published by prototype in 2019.

Nathan Dragon has been published in *NOON Annual, Fence*, and *New York Tyrant*. Dragon is from (and currently in) Salem, MA working on a book of fictions.

Sarah Boulton is an artist based in Mid-Wales. Her first collection, *Continuum*, was recently published with Care of Time.

Sascha Macht was born in Frankfurt (Oder) and studied at the German Institute for Literature in Leipzig. He has published prose, poetry, and drama in various anthologies and literary magazines. He has received fellowships from Künstlerhaus Lukas, Ahrenshoop, the Cultural Foundation of the Free State of Saxony, the Literary Colloquium Berlin, the Schloss Wiepersdorf Cultural Foundation, and the German Literature Fund. His first novel, *The War in the Garden of the King of the Dead,* was published by DuMont in spring 2016. From 2013 to 2017, he was a research associate at the German Institute for Literature in Leipzig, investigating the education of writers in the GDR. In 2018, together with Isabelle Lehn and Katja Stopka, he published *Learning to Write in Socialism: The Johannes R. Becher Institute for Literature.* He lives in Leipzig.

Hannah Regel Hannah Regel is an artist based in London. She holds a BA in art practice from Goldsmiths College and a MFA in sculpture from the Slade School of Fine Art. Her writing has been published in *Eros Journal, Two Serious Ladies, Leste Magazine, Montez Press Interjection Calendar, The Literateur, Form IV* and *The Laboratory for Aesthetics and Ecology.* Her first chapbook of poetry, *When I Was Alive*, was published in 2017, and her first collection *Oliver Reed* in 2020, both releases from Montez Press. She is also co-editor of the feminist journal SALT.

Andrew Lampert's irrelevance has been commented upon by all who have ever been in a position to judge him for inclusion or advancement. Sizable disinterest in his extensive body of films, videos, photos and performances quadruples each year. Occasional errors in judgment and clerical mistakes have led to his works appearing in numerous international museums, festivals and venues, but the global powers that be have redoubled their efforts to prevent this from ever happening again. He has been allowed to edit books of other people's writings and art because their work is so much better than his. *Hotel*, in their infinite pity, accepted Lampert's overwrought contribution to this issue, which took him a considerable amount of time to write, although no one would ever guess that from reading it.

Emmanuel Iduma is the author of *A Stranger's Pose*, which was longlisted for the 2019 Ondaatje Prize, and *The Sound of Things to Come*, a novel. His essays on art and photography have appeared, most recently, in *The New York Review of Books, Art in America, BOMB, Off Assignment* and *LitHub*. He teaches at the School of Visual Arts, New York.

Lotte LS is a poet living in Great Yarmouth, the furthest easterly outlier of England.

Amanda DeMarco is a translator living in Berlin.

0x0a is a text collective for digital conceptual literature comprising Gregor Weichbrodt and Hannes Bajohr.

Hannah Williams is a writer and editor based in London. Her work has appeared in *Granta, The Guardian, Artsy, GARAGE* and more, and she was named runner-up in Boulevard's 2019 Short Fiction Contest for New Writers. She is currently working on her first novel and tweets at @hkatewilliams.

Lauren de Sá Naylor is an artist, poet, educator and bartender based in Todmorden, West Yorkshire. Her poetic, essay writing & AV practice is discursive and interdisciplinary, meandering between text, image and documentary, coalescing around the idea of thinking-as-writing and negotiation with the psyche. Lauren is concerned with reading and writing in their broadest possible sense, the production of subjectivity and the poetics of relation, an interwoven approach to thinking and the proximity of articulation to the body, the erotic and haptic perception. Lauren has published dream manuscripts widely and reads texts live in audio-visual performances, sometimes in collaboration.

Jen Calleja is a writer and literary translator. Her short story collection *I'm Afraid That's All We've Got Time For* was published by Prototype. Her translation of Marion Poschmann's *The Pine Islands* was shortlisted for the Man Booker International Prize 2019.

Cass McCombs is a musician from Northern California, whose latest album is *Tip of the Sphere*.

Rachel Genn formerly a neuroscientist, has written two novels: *The Cure* (2011), and *What You Could Have Won* (2020). She was Leverhulme Artist-in-Residence (2006), University of Sheffield, creating a quasi-institution called THE NATIONAL FACILITY FOR THE REGULATION OF REGRET, spanning installation art, VR and film (ASFF 2016), presented together at SXSW, 2017. She has written for *Granta, 3AM* and *The Real Story* and is currently working on a long essay on immersion in the creative act as well as a collection of non-fictions about fighting and addiction to regret (2019–2020).

Emmanuelle Pagano was born in Rodez (Aveyron) in 1969. Her novels have been translated into more than a dozen languages, and she has won multiple awards for her writing, including the EU Prize for Literature and most recently the French Ecology Novel Prize. Her first book published in English, *Trysting* was published by And Other Stories in 2016; her second, *Faces on the Tip of my Tongue*, was published by Peirene Press in 2019.

Sophie Lewis is an editor and translator from French and Portuguese. Her recent translations include books by Colette Fellous, Emmanuelle Pagano and Leïla Slimani.

Jennifer Higgins is a translator from French and Italian. She has translated several works of fiction including *Trysting* and *Faces on the Tip of my Tongue* by Emmanuelle Pagano. Recent projects include *A Short Philosophy of Birds* by Philippe Dubois and Elise Rousseau, and she is currently translating *The Photographer of Auschwitz* by Luca Crippo and Maurizio Onnis. Jennifer's translations have appeared in *3:AM Magazine*, *Lit Hub*, *Volupté* and *Sonofabook Magazine*, among others. She is also Assistant Director of the Queen's College Translation Exchange.

Lauren Elkin is a Franco-American writer, critic, and translator. Most recently she is the author of *Flâneuse: Women Walk the City* (Chatto & Windus).

Clemens Meyer was born 1977 in Halle and lives in Leipzig. After high school he jobbed as a watchman, building worker and removal man. He studied creative writing at the German Institute for Literature, Leipzig and was granted a scholarship by the Saxon Ministry of Science and Arts in 2002. *Bricks and Mortar*, his latest novel, was shortlisted for the German Book Prize, awarded the Bremer Literaturpreis 2014, longlisted for the 2017 Man Booker International Prize, and shortlisted for the 2019 Best Translated Book Awards. A collection of short stories, *Dark Satellites*, was published by Fitzcarraldo Editions in 2020.

Katy Derbyshire, originally from London, has lived in Berlin for over twenty years. She translates contemporary German writers including Inka Parei, Heike Geissler, Olga Grjasnowa, Annett Gröschner and Christa Wolf. Her translation of Clemens Meyer's *Bricks and Mortar* was the winner of the 2018 Straelener Übersetzerpreis (Straelen Prize for Translation). She occasionally teaches translation and also co-hosts a monthly translation lab and the bi-monthly Dead Ladies Show.

Hotel #6

Spring, 2020

partisanhotel.co.uk

Hotel is a magazine for new approaches to fiction, non-fiction and poetry.

The epigraph is excerpted from **Wayne Koestenbaum**'s archive, recently acquired by **Yal Beinecke Rare Book & Manuscript Library** in 2019 (CT, USA)—*"Over the course of a vari and prolific career, Wayne Koestenbaum has published poetry collections, volumes of cultur criticism, novels, and a libretto. Two years ago, he plunged into an entirely different sort of pr ject, one that involved managing Excel spreadsheets and contemplating his unpublished wor Yale's Beinecke Rare Book & Manuscript Library has acquired Koestenbaum's literary archi As part of the acquisition, Koestenbaum offered to help process his papers so they could available to researchers more quickly. He has provided the library with spreadsheets of inform tion detailed enough to guide scholars through hundreds of folders of correspondence, journa notes, drafts, unpublished work, photographs, and ephemera dating back to his childhood."*

Astrid Alben's poems 'Collateral Damage,' 'The First People' (*for Marlene Dumas*), 'Copi Strategies,' 'Words to Say it' and 'God Became a Monkey' (*for Hannah Höch*) are excerpt from the collection ***Plainspeak*** published by **prototype** (2019). © Astrid Alben, 2019. Th work is reproduced in **Hotel** by permission of **prototype**, London.

Hannah Regel's poems 'Making Sausages,' 'Mermaid Outing,' 'Butterfield' and 'Marissa' a excerpted from her collection ***Oliver Reed***, published by **Montez Press** (2020). © Hann Regel, 2020. This work is reproduced in **Hotel** by permission of the author.

Cass McCombs' poems 'A Public Mural' and 'The Truck Driver & Malverde' are except from the collection ***Toy Fabels***—an illustrated book of poetry published by **Spurl Editio** (2019). Text, illustrations and photography © Cass McCombs, 2019. This work is reproduc in **Hotel** by permission of **Spurl Editions**, Sacramento, CA.

Rachel Genn's essay 'Dreamy Idiotic Visions of the Future' is an adapted iteration of a wo first delivered during the proceedings of **'Love Takes Risks'**—a symposium on the poetics a practices of contemporary small-press fiction. Hosted at the University of East Anglia (N wich, UK) on 2nd March 2019, the symposium was organised by Olivia Heal and Rosali Brown in the School of Literature, Drama and Creative Writing, and hosted by the **UI Publishing Project** and the **Republic of Consciousness**—a prize celebrating achievement small-press publishing.

Emmanuelle Pagano's short story 'The Automatic Tour Guide' is excerpted from the c lection *Faces on the Tip of my Tongue* (Peirene Press, 2019). © Emmanuelle Pagano, 20 English translation copyright © Jennifer Higgins and Sophie Lewis, 2020. ***Faces on the Tip my Tongue*** (*Un renard á mains nues*) was originally published in French by POL Editeur 2012. This work is reproduced in **Hotel** by permission of **Peirene Press**, London.

auren **Elkin**'s 'Silent B' is excerpted from the pamphlet project ***Detour/Détours***—the first ›llection in the **Hotel Cordel** series, co-published with the independent press **Les Fugitives.** ıe collection gathers together a set of specially commissioned texts and translations that address our various definitions of debt. ***Detour/Détours*** imagines debt as a language game: a broken pun; a break in a journey; a play on value and the meaning of money as it changes ands. Participating authors were given free rein to produce a piece of writing in response these ideas, and the works included herein—five first English-language translations and ve original texts—wind their way around the weight of the word 'debt' in ten attempts reroute its meaning. Edited by Emmanuel Bouju, Dominic Jaeckle and Cécile Menon, ***etour/Détours*** features texts and translations from **Noémi Lefebvre, Natacha Lasorak, ›phie Lewis, Mathieu Larnaudie, Adrian Nathan West, Selma Dabbagh, Preti Taneja, ındra Lucbert, Jessica Spivey, Jen Calleja, Nicolas Bouyssi, Amanda DeMarco, Joanna 'alsh, Thomas Clerc** and **Jeffrey Zuckerman** alongside **Elkin.** ***Detour/Détours*** is distributed :clusively **by Hotel** and **Les Fugitives**, and—designed and typeset by **Niall Reynolds**—was inted in a limited edition of 300 copies by TJ International in January 2020.

lemens Meyer's 'The Return of the Argonauts' is excerpted from *Dark Satellites* (Fitzcarraldo litions, 2020). © Clemens Meyer, 2020; English translation copyright © Katy Derbyshire, 20; ***Dark Satellites (Die stillen Trabanten)*** was originally published in German by S. Fischer 2017. This work is reproduced in **Hotel** by permission of **Fitzcarraldo Editions**, London.

l other works appear in **Hotel** for the first time.

otel would like to thank **Jess Chandler, Eva Richter, Dan Levy, Stella Sabin, Cécile Menon, cques Testard** and **Clare Bogen** for all their assistance, aid and support.

---

otel is edited by **Jon Auman, Thomas Chadwick & Dominic Jaeckle** and designed and peset by **Niall Reynolds.**

r all enquiries, including submissions, subscriptions and distribution, please email us at **itors@partisanhotel.co.uk**

BN 978-1-8380200-0-2

Printed in Poland
by Amazon Fulfillment
Poland Sp. z o.o., Wrocław

58068298R00127